LOUD AS BONES

DG WOODS

Loud as Bones by D. G. Woods

Published in the United States of America by

Cabins Press LLC

ISBN-13: 979-8-9920445-6-0 (Paperback edition)

ISBN-13: 979-8-9920445-5-3 (Ebook edition)

First Edition: June 15, 2026

Printed in the United States of America

LOUD AS BONES

From my nightmares to yours.
Happy haunting.

a novella

Loud as Bones

DG Woods

It is a terrifying thing, how adaptable the human spirit is. We can grow accustomed to almost any horror, provided it arrives in increments. We stay because we loathe the rupture of change more than the ache of our own undoing.

TRIGGER WARNINGS

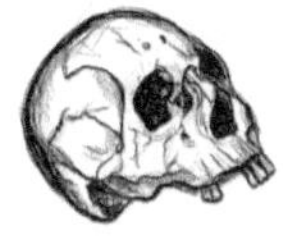

- Graphic violence & gore (blood, mutilation, body parts described in detail)
- Body horror
- Cannibalism
- Murder & death
- Torture
- Psychological horror
- Coercion
- Disturbing imagery
- Suicidal ideation
- Agoraphobia
- SA
- Post-mortem body mutilation
- Animal injury (no graphic detail)
- Animal death

I

Night fell unexpectedly, like a trapdoor giving way beneath the day.

Sylvie came home from work, her car engine coughing once before dying in the driveway, but she didn't come upstairs to say hello. She was in the kitchen, rifling through drawers and cabinets for something to eat. She found nothing. I hadn't cooked. I hadn't shopped. I had done nothing at all. Instead, I remained tethered to my desk, agonizing over commas and em dashes, only to delete more than I'd written. I was finally drafting the vampire novel—a dream I'd frenzied over since high school but buried because my first girlfriend said vampires were passé, and my work would never amount to anything. I had always been attracted to the snobby, scholarly type, the kind of people who looked at my aspirations only to criticize them.

Now that I finally had the time to write, the words wouldn't come.

The back door opened and shut with a click. Sylvie retreated to the backyard for a smoke. There, the white swing on the tree quivered like a dead body next to the off-white gazebo, a sun-bleached ruin slowly collapsing into itself.

I wanted to preserve it. All of it, but mainly the gazebo. We would have to restore it, but I loved it even in its decay. I loved all things abandoned and left to fend for themselves, and this gazebo was exactly that. It spoke to me.

Sylvie, however, was determined to tear it down. She hated gazebos. When asked why, she would shrug and say they served no sensible purpose other than crowding the yard. If you wanted shade, you could sit beneath a tree or on the porch, and if it rained, what good was a gazebo anyway? You would still have to walk through the downpour, soaked to the skin, just to reach the bathroom. To her, it was a pointless structure.

Perhaps she was right. Gazebos were limited in function. But this one was likely a century old, as old as the house itself. Real wood, crafted with care and mastery that modern craftsmen wouldn't waste time on. It gave the house its gothic charm, that faint sense of something forgotten, delicate, and romantic. I told Sylvie it would photograph beautifully when restored, that guests at our B&B would post about it and tag us. She liked that idea, so she let it stay. "For now."

What I didn't tell her—what I would never say aloud—was that I hoped she might one day propose to me in that very gazebo. Freshly painted. Draped in ivy. Wrapped in dusk. I would wear the dress she liked, the light blue one that floated when I walked, and I would cry, overwhelmed.

Or, more realistically, I would be in sweatpants and a paint-streaked Nightmare on Elm Street T-shirt, hands rough from sanding and scrubbing, and she would slip a ring onto a finger with chipped nails and flecks of dirt.

But I would be happy all the same.

A proposal would mean the end of the vicious fights that had swallowed our first year in Whitmore House (I loved that it had a name). It would mean our money troubles had finally loosened their grip, and the house had been given a new lease on life. Most of all, it would mean our relationship had drifted back to its gentler shape: back to the early days when we'd just moved in, when we couldn't walk past each other without bruising our skin, losing ourselves in that frantic, open-mouthed hunger. It would mean we were speaking, truly speaking, and the first thing she'd do after coming home from work was climb the stairs to kiss me and ask how my writing was going. I would tell her everything I had written that day: tales of vampires and damsels, concubines and crumbling castles, curses and blood-lit halls, all while she made me pant, forcing the words out of me as I struggled to breathe.

When we decided to leave the city, trading the noise of the busy streets for the silence and the views of the Hudson Valley, we knew we were looking for a fixer-upper. We sifted through dozens of condemned "investor's dreams" before we finally found the one.

The house had passed through many hands, bearing a palimpsest of change throughout the years, but I had a vision for the property. I believed we could restore it, return it to its former stature until it once again bore its name with pride: Whitmore House.

The property's final hook was a wine cellar left behind by the previous owners, but the agent couldn't find the key to the heavy iron padlock on the floor hatch. Sylvie and I never saw what lay beneath.

"We'll crack it when we're ready to renovate," she said.

I thought of Bluebeard's forbidden room, and I prayed the cellar didn't hold a harvest of dead wives.

At the town hall, an unsmiling woman behind the counter—the kind who thrives on giving unsolicited advice—warned us (or possibly cursed us) with her doomed thoughts on homeownership. We were there to pull the records and check for liens, giddy and loud, telling anyone who would listen that we were the proud owners of a bewitching Victorian. She listened without interest before hissing, "Just be prepared. Those first five years make or break you. Houses love to fall apart all at once."

I laughed it off then, but her words proved truer than any prophecy.

Two months after closing, I lost my job. At first, it didn't feel catastrophic. We had renovation money set aside, and I was certain I would find new work—even more certain my book would sell.

It did not. Nor did any jobs materialize—not for someone with a degree in communications, anyway. We had moved into the middle of nowhere, and career opportunities were as scarce as the winter sun.

Back in the city, I worked as an event coordinator. But once we settled, the firm cut me loose, despite their initial promises of remote work.

"Out of sight, out of mind," Sylvie sighed.

She had changed jobs and had taken a pay cut to move here with me. Now, she still had to commute for over an hour to Kingston, but at least her place in the professional world was secure. Everyone needed accountants. No one needed people who existed in the spaces between things.

Our savings thinned to almost nothing. And as the months passed, the house began revealing problems neither the agent nor the inspector had mentioned, as if it had waited for us to settle in before showing its true nature. The foundation. The mold. The roof. We could simply not keep up.

Sylvie started working from the office more, even though her firm had no strict rules about it. I suspected she preferred the cold fluorescent light of her cubicle and the forced small talk of her colleagues to being entombed in this money pit with me.

And then she finally admitted she had never wanted any of

it. Not the house. Not the land. Not the stillness of the wide, empty fields, nor the star-soaked nights and the quiet that settled like a weighted blanket. She never wanted to leave the city, never wanted to change jobs, and certainly never wanted to pour her life and savings into restoring a "shitty old house" for people who thought a weekend in the middle of nowhere counted as luxury. She had done it for me—and realized, too late, it was a mistake.

We hadn't spoken for days after that fight. When a thin semblance of communication did return, the air between us was too poisoned. She began coming home later and later, offering hollow corporate excuses before I could even ask: "year-end close," "the audit trail." They sounded like a foreign language in these harrowed halls. She wouldn't look at me when she said them.

Then she would retreat downstairs behind a closed door, leaving me in a silence broken only by Whitmore groaning in its slumber.

Sylvie also developed the habit of waiting until Morpheus had claimed me before slipping into our bed. She'd even tried staying in a separate bedroom—the only other space with a mattress, tucked away on the third floor where we barely went. We kept it for unexpected guests, though my estranged family didn't even know where I lived, and Sylvie's parents were long gone.

I hated the physical distance she was forcing between us. I hated that she no longer wanted to share *our* bed. Eventually, I tricked her into coming back, claiming I'd had a nightmare where she died and that I couldn't bear another night alone. I even cried until we made up.

But since then, she had been more distant than ever. She refused to discuss the estrangement between us, and I existed in a state of suspension, never knowing what to expect and with no one to turn to for advice.

I took to wandering the vast, empty grounds, desperate to escape the solitude pressing in from every corner of the estate. And worst of all, unlike her, I had nowhere else to go. With Sylvie at work, and us having only one vehicle as we couldn't afford another, I was trapped.

And before long, I settled into the rot, a comfortable shroud of our life at Whitmore House, preferring the predictable chill of Sylvie's muteness to the terrifying uncertainty of an exit I couldn't bring myself to find. I became a useless ghost, haunting the corridors, following her from room to room, unnoticed, hoping that one day things might return to the way they once were.

II

Whitmore woke me with agonizing urgency.

Disoriented, I lay trembling, unsure whether the vibration came from me or from the ground itself. The front door opened with a pained groan. Then a voice—a woman's. It was clear, terrifyingly close, and stripped of the electronic tin of a speakerphone. I turned to the clock: 2:14 a.m.

Sylvie responded to our visitor, but unlike the stranger, her words were muffled and anxious.

I sat up, unease coiling cold and taut along my spine. Who could it be? We had no neighbors for miles. It was what had initially drawn us here: a quiet so profound it felt sacred. Hidden behind the forest, the road to the estate left to ruin, Whitmore House was not a place anyone stumbled upon by accident. You had to be looking for it. Or you had to be invited.

Sylvie's voice shifted, sharp now, and she screamed, "No!"

Glass shattered. A heavy crash followed. Then a violent, structural bang that shook the very foundation.

I lurched to my feet, dizzy with panic, trying to shake off the last remnants of sleep and wrest control of my body. I scanned the room for anything I could lift, swing, or use to defend myself. The heavy old wardrobe, not built-in. A matching chest of drawers. Two armchairs. A lamp. The bed. I cursed silently that we didn't own a gun, or at least a baseball bat.

The violence below reached a crescendo before receding. They were outside now.

I reached the window in time to see Sylvie, barefoot, sprinting across the lawn. Her robe trailed behind her like the wings of a broken bird as she vanished where the porch light failed. I pressed my face to the glass, peering into the night to see who was after her. No one came out. Her frantic screams continued to tear through the dark, but no one was chasing her.

What was happening?

Inside the house, everything suddenly settled. The grandfather clock in the hall took up the slack, its metronome tick-tick-ticking at an artificially slow pace. Was someone still in here with me? If so, they weren't moving. I knew the anatomy of Whitmore—the specific, splintering groan of the third step, the hollow rattle of the ceramic slabs in the kitchen. No one could move through these withered arteries without announcing themselves.

I pried open the bedroom door, careful to avoid the creak, and stepped into the hallway. Biting air nipped my skin, and the floorboards protested under my weight as I crept downstairs. Each sound felt magnified, but I could do little to suppress the old wood. Sylvie needed help.

The kitchen was empty. The back door yawned wide open, admitting the damp exhale of the night. Beside it, everything looked normal, which made it feel all the more wrong: the way a single cupboard door hung ajar, the bruised fruit in the bowl, the scattered breadcrumbs on the counter. It all felt like the scene of a crime yet to happen. I stepped back from the exit.

Pain sliced through my foot.

Glass protruded from the sensitive arch, and I bit back a cry. Walking on my heels, I limped across the room and yanked a handful of paper towels from the counter, crouching to remove the shard. My fingers shook as I stifled the blood, and my throat was so tight I thought I would pass out. I couldn't stand the sight of blood.

Fragments of broken plates were scattered across the tiles. They had been sitting on the counter for days. We had taken the cabinets down weeks ago to start renovating, but we never went any further than tearing things apart and covering them in plastic. I had the time now that I didn't have a day job, but not the skills. That had always been Sylvie's strength.

Then I heard it.

Footsteps.

Not mine.

Not Sylvie's.

Beyond the exposed kitchen lath, in the black of the adjacent rooms, someone was displacing the silence. The soft ripple reminded me of wading through water. I froze, every muscle rigid. My heartbeat thrashed so hard it hurt.

Whoever this woman was, she hadn't chased Sylvie, and that thought alone made me feel slightly better. Perhaps Sylvie could hide and call for help.

But she didn't scare easily. If she ran, it was for a reason. A weapon? If the intruder was armed, I had to be ready. I needed a way to protect myself long before any help could arrive.

My instinct screamed at me to flee, but I stayed, tethered by the need to find Sylvie or call 911.

My phone was upstairs, abandoned in the panic.

I cursed silently.

Heavenly Father, if we survive this, I'll change. I'll install the alarms. I'll stop relying on the remoteness of the estate to protect us.

Today, the isolation was a betrayal.

There was a chef's knife forgotten in the sink. My hand

gripped the handle, my palm slick with sweat. The weapon felt too light, too thin, against the unknown.

But it was all I had.

As I shifted, a loose tile clattered.

Whoever plagued the sanctity of Whitmore had surely heard me through its weakening walls.

Then, the steps: loud, fast, someone sprinting.

Fuck, fuck, fuck.

In my haste, I stepped on glass again. The sliver bit deep, carving worse than the last. Hot blood colored the slats like glittering jewels.

I bolted for the back door, no longer caring if I was heard, or about my phone—only my own safety. But as I approached it, the murk on the other side of the glass curdled. A silhouette materialized out of the night, cutting off my exit.

Someone impossibly tall and bulky, their shape distorted by gloom and fog. Male. The woman hadn't come alone, of course; this was a planned attack. But that wasn't the worst part.

The giant figure dragged a limp body behind him like a broken toy.

Sylvie.

Her skin was a deathly, translucent pale, her hair tangled into a matted crown of thorns. Her eyes were closed, her mouth hanging open, and her arms stretched above her head as the beast hauled her through the dirt. I couldn't tell if she was still alive.

I collapsed to my knees, pushing myself backward over the glass. The grinding of grit and skin made my pulse race. I had to get out of there. I had to—

Panic was a suffocating kiss. I scrambled, dragging myself from the kitchen before being noticed. My vision had tunneled to a single point, my route: living room, hall, front door—the only path to safety. Miles of road didn't matter. I needed to get help. The police. Anything. The only thing that mattered was breaking the threshold and reaching the night.

Then, a shadow passed the entrance like a wraith. It didn't even turn to acknowledge me. *No, no, no, no, no.*

Someone was in the living room, cutting off my escape.

It must have been the woman I'd heard, the one Sylvie had spoken with. My legs locked, but momentum propelled me forward. I stumbled, fell, and the knife clattered to the floor.

A pause—then movement elsewhere in the house. That sound didn't go unnoticed.

I snatched it up, grateful I hadn't landed on the blade, and dodged toward the nearest doorway—the downstairs bathroom. The plumbing was dead, long forgotten. The door stayed slightly ajar, just enough for them to think the escape route continued toward the front of the house.

Carefully, I stepped into the basin. It yawned beneath me, a porcelain coffin deep enough to swallow me whole. I remained upright, nudging the yellowed curtain just enough to blur my outline. Stagnant air filled my lungs, heavy with rust and mildew.

I froze, straining my ears.

Every tiny sound swelled. It threaded through the walls. It bored into my skull.

Step. Step. Step.

Bare feet on the cold floor. Closer.

Step. Step.

A pause. The floor whined under their weight. Then, the tempo shifted.

Step. Step. Pause. Step. Pause.

Further away.

Tears carved hot trails down my cheeks. Nothing existed beyond this night, this need to endure, to cling to the thin, trembling thread of life inside me. I just wanted to live.

Please, let me live. I just want to live. I'll be good, God. I'll change. Just let me live.

I forced my breathing into a steady rhythm: inhale, hold, exhale. Repeat. Repeat. Repeat. It worked. Calm replaced panic, the space around me sharpened, and a plan began to form.

The knife steadied in my grip. I was ready to protect myself. To attack. To fight. To kill. Whatever it took to survive. Whatever it took to save Sylvie.

I turned my attention outward once more.

Seconds passed. Or minutes. Or hours. The dark hummed with impatience. Time had unraveled completely. I existed only in the now, fear a drumbeat beneath my skin. Then timber shifted.

Just outside the bathroom.

They'd found me.

A soft creak. The door inched open. It was quiet enough to pretend it wasn't real. But I knew better. It wasn't just a draft. It was someone moving, carefully testing the silence for weak spots.

I couldn't stand it any longer, couldn't stay there waiting to be found. With a cry that tore itself free from my chest, I lunged from the tub, the curtain tangling around me like a funeral shroud.

My body collided with the woman in the doorway. We crashed together. I could see the pale blur of her face and the frantic, serpentine thrash of her limbs beneath me. She was stronger than she looked. I struggled to keep her down. I needed to act fast.

With every grain of will I had, I drove the steel home. The blade punctured the curtain, finding her throat. The yellow fabric masked everything but the wound, making it look like a surgery—a body draped and prepped for incision.

It didn't slide in clean. There was resistance as it grated against cartilage and shoved through something hard. Blood began to pour, black in the absence of light. A gasp tore out of her, a wet, choking sound that bubbled and died in her throat.

She clawed at the curtain, trying to rip it away, but the more she struggled, the more the fabric tangled around her. *Die, I thought, or maybe screamed. Just fucking die already!*

Flailing now, hands cutting through the air in blind, desperate arcs. I didn't flinch. I kept the knife pressed in, leaning my weight into her.

Yet, her body refused to still. She was still fighting me. Through the partition, two black coals burned with a pure concentration of hate.

Why wouldn't she die?

God, die. Die!

I screamed the word internally and shoved the steel deeper. Her lips peeled back from her teeth in a terrible grimace.

There was so much blood. It was everywhere, slicking the tiles, coating my hands, soaking into the bath mat. All I could think of was Sylvie. I needed to find her. I needed to know if she still lived.

The tension rod finally snapped under our combined weight, striking the side of my head with a metallic crack. Stars burst across my vision. I didn't know a human skull could sound so hollow.

Involuntarily, I loosened my hold on the knife, and the advantage I held over her began to shift.

Hold it together! You've almost got her!

Then the memory struck like a lightning bolt—the man, the tall monster hauling Sylvie by the leg. My body recoiled on instinct.

But it wasn't just the memory that hit me.

It was *him*.

Fingers tangled in my hair and yanked with a strength that sent me hurtling. I hit the porcelain hard. The back of my ribs took the force, and the air fled my chest. I slumped against the tub, gasping.

An unnatural cold poured from the man, spreading through the room like frost claiming a tomb. When he leaned closer, his long obsidian hair fell forward, the ends grazing my cheeks like the feathers of a dead bird, softly illuminated by the light spilling in from the hallway.

For a moment, I was certain Death itself had come to collect me.

A primitive terror opened its black maw and pulled me into its center. My limbs turned soft and useless. The cold tiles pressed into my skin. The world started to fade, and I struggled to gather my thoughts, my mind already swimming, slipping loose.

He let go of my hair, turning away to kneel over the woman. With slow, careful movements, he unwrapped her from the curtain. I watched them in a trance, captivated by the grotesque sight of two bloodied strangers in my home.

It's a dream. Just a bad dream.

I almost laughed. Of course it wasn't real. It couldn't be. But the dead weight of dread in my chest didn't go away.

"Help me," the woman croaked, convulsing on the floor.

How could she still speak? The knife still jutted from her neck.

He wrapped one hand around the handle, the other pressing against her shoulder in a vice. And pulled.

A guttural roar erupted from her as the blade slid free. Blood surged in a violent wave. It poured over her breasts, splashed to the floor, and painted him red.

And then, impossibly, she sat up.

The skin writhed and peeled apart beneath her fingers, reopening the jagged wound with every twitch and shudder. She looked at me again, fuming, but too weak to exact revenge.

The man followed her gaze toward me. His face was long

and still, but it was his eyes that held me. They were empty and endless, like twin voids that devoured light and hope alike.

The woman looked at me, too, and all I saw was a blood-smeared monster with a crevice where her throat should have been. She rose to her feet and smiled, and the wound beneath her chin tore into a cruel grin of its own—splitting and splitting until it eclipsed her face entirely. Soon, all I could see was that black, widening mouth stitching with the night itself.

III

The light outside was the soft gold of late afternoon, but something about it felt wrong. The stillness of a snow globe scene, a frozen, plastic perfection that lasted only until someone lifted the world and shook it. I stood by the window, seeking a moment of apricity to thaw the chill that settled deep in my bones. Dust suspended in the beams slanting through the apertures, drifting like ash. Through the glass, I saw Sylvie's car pull into the driveway.

She stepped out slowly, keys jangling in her hand. By the way she shut the door (a single, irritated motion), I already knew. She was in a mood. A bad one.

I fluttered with nervous anticipation. How could I fix it? What could I do to make it better?

Things had been strange for weeks. She didn't talk to me anymore. When she did, it was always a list of things she didn't like about me, and it usually ended in raised voices and one of us retreating behind a locked door.

I scrambled mentally, trying to figure out why she would be upset with me this time.

A thought pressed against the edge of my mind, but I

couldn't quite catch it. Something forgotten. Something I couldn't name. It slinked just beyond reach like a shadow crawling along the wall, slipping away when I tried to look at it, creeping closer every time I turned away. I felt it in the pit of my stomach, down to my very core. It was dark. Oh, how dark it was.

And I was so very afraid to remember.

I knew that once I caught it, everything would change. There would be no more light. No more love.

The air curdled, and my lungs stalled. A low hum filled my ears, like bees trapped in the walls. The house whimpered and shifted, uncomfortable. Shadows stretched long and unnatural across the floor. My body began to shake, though I wasn't cold. It was a dread that trapped me like roots.

I wanted to run to Sylvie. To call out and tell her not to come in. To warn her. To tell her to leave before it was too late.

But I couldn't move.

The memory—whatever it was—pressed down on me like a tombstone. Somewhere in the house, a door opened with an ominous creak.

And then the light began to fade.

The smell came first.

Sharp, metallic, coppery. Biological. So intense it seemed to have penetrated every pocket of oxygen, replacing the air with a thick, iron weight. I had cut my hand on a switchblade once, and the mess had smelled exactly like this. Only now, the stench was a thousand times stronger. Beneath it, sour threads of piss and sweat coiled upward. A stench of bodies reduced to their most primitive, animal state.

My head throbbed. Each beat felt like something trying to break out. My arms would not obey, heavy and aching in their sockets, like they had been forcibly removed from me and loosely reattached.

It was all coming back in uneven bursts. The strangers. The woman with the gash across her throat. Red hair plastered with gore. The knife in my hand. Sylvie.

Sylvie!

I sat up like something possessed from the grave, but my resurrection was brief. A violent tug yanked my arms backward, sawing bone.

The sound came second. I heard it now, what had been there all along. A percussion. Slapping, obscene. Low gasps breaking the air, throats working with effort and release, skin dragging against skin. The sound of two bodies locked together, panting, moving.

And beneath it, something else. The sound was hard to separate from the pounding inside my head, but the longer I lay there, the clearer it became. The noise was coming from outside.

Music.

Not in this room, but rising from somewhere below, from the speakers Sylvie had bought. It was too loud. A deformity. A blunt insult to the style of Whitmore. She listened to the kind of music I despised—some strain of techno. Now, its synthetic breath filled the room with a relentless, vibrating thrum that melded with the sounds from the bed—the moans, the sucking, the sharp knock of flesh. Madness in stereo.

My throat constricted into a dry knot as panic scraped against my ribs. I closed my eyes, praying it was a nightmare.

It wasn't. It remained, no matter how fiercely I pleaded to wake.

I tried to focus. I needed something steady to cling to, but the room refused me. It tilted. It stretched. It warped around me. The dark was not empty; it shifted and gathered, taking on wobbly shapes before dispersing them like a swarm of flies.

This was our bedroom—mine and Sylvie's. The sheets, the dresser, and the canvas featuring our first holiday over the bed. Her perfume bottles were still neatly aligned on the vanity, ordered by expense, not by favour, because Sylvie always shoved what she didn't like out of sight.

But it all looked unbearably wrong.

The only light came from the night lamp. Sylvie had thrown a strip of red fabric over it after reading something about ambience in Elle. Crimson pooled over the walls, soaked the rug, slicked the bed. Everything looked flayed open. Not a room, but the stomach of some great beast. I felt as if I were being digested alive.

I blinked hard, certain the color would thin, that sense would reassemble. But it only thickened until the world itself shrank into a pulsing red haze.

Shadows writhed on the bed, their shapes tangled and perverse. For a heartbeat, I thought they were hurting Sylvie, tearing her apart, but when my eyes adjusted, I saw it was them —the man and the woman with the slit throat. How was she still alive? How could she still move?

Oh God. She was not just alive.

They were fucking. Vigorously.

Their bodies writhed and twisted. She was on top now. For a moment, I thought she wore a skin-tight bodysuit, something glossy and slick, until I realized she was completely naked, drenched in a glistening, cranberry sheen. The lower half of her face looked like it had been dipped in paint, her lips and chin smeared and shining in the lamp's suffocated glow. The gape in her throat was hidden beneath a silk scarf, the edges stained like bruises.

Blood shone on her chest, streaking her lover's skin as she moved. She let out small, fractured sounds, fragile and almost childlike, interrupted only by the occasional guttural groans of the man.

I twisted once, uselessly.

The chains around my wrists trailed back and locked around the radiator—old metal pipes from another century, built heavy and indestructible.

A shift rippled across the bed. I thought the man was slipping, his body sliding from beneath her thighs. But no—they kept moving, rutting, as if nothing in the world was out of place. The shift continued, and then, with heavy, graceless weight, something fell off the bed, crashing to the floor.

A body.

The scream that tore out of me did not sound human. It dragged itself from my throat until my vocal cords were ribbons of scalded, weeping grit.

Because the body lying crumpled on the floor was Sylvie.

I reached toward her, helpless, my arms cut short. Sylvie's limbs contorted at impossible angles, her face barely recognizable. Eyes open, unblinking. Mouth frozen in mid-scream. Sylvie was naked, her skin crosshatched with raw cuts. She was coated in a dark film of blood. I wrenched and twisted, but the chains were merciless.

I wanted to claw at myself, peel away my skin, gouge out my eyes, shatter my ears—anything to smother the roaring in my skull. I wanted to disappear from every sense, to stop existing in every way.

All I had left was to scream, and scream, and scream, staring into Sylvie's dead eyes.

The figures on our bed ignored me entirely. They moved in their own filth, lost in their frenzy, treating me like nothing more than a harmless spectre thrashing in the sullied light. Like they were accustomed to it.

The woman with the scarf shrieked, a high, piercing sound that tore through the room. Her entire body convulsed and shook while he held her against himself, seeking his own release. At last, their violent ecstasy ended. He lay splayed across the sheets, limbs slack, his form melting into the gloom. Even from here, the man looked enormous next to this subtle woman; the bed was barely long enough for him. She slid off him, and his male organ leaned sideways, winking in the hue of the lamp.

They had been rutting in Sylvie's blood.

My stomach clenched.

The woman rose from the bed and stepped over the pile that had once been the love of my life. In her bloodied nudity, beneath the scarf at her neck, she wore a large medallion that nestled between the smooth swell of her breasts. I was perplexed as she advanced toward me, all feline grace and feral eyes. She showed no sign of pain or discomfort. I must not have cut her as deep as I thought. Maybe I dreamt it all—the knife slicing through her throat, the struggle, the fight. Maybe it ended before I realized it had ended.

Turning to Sylvie's vanity, her hand hovered before plucking something small and silver from its surface. A sharp click split the air. A Stanley knife.

She looked at me. And her eyes—*God, her eyes.* They were feverish pinpricks, the eyes of a madwoman.

Oh God. She means to do it.

The knife wasn't strong or long enough to kill me instantly. It would be slow, miserable, a punishment for what I had done to her.

Death by a million cuts.

Her grip was iron. I writhed like a trapped feral cat, spitting and jerking against her hold, but she didn't give an inch. She drew the knife across my wrist, and the flesh yielded under the blade. Pain burst through me in a blinding white bloom. My essence oozed from the open seam of my wrist, hot and syrupy.

She held my arm outstretched, pinning it down, then, almost tenderly, brushed the damp curls away from her face.

"Shh," she whispered, lips forming a soft, coaxing pout. I felt like a frightened child being soothed by a fairy tale witch who was checking the fat on their victim. "You bleed so pretty."

Her mouth met my skin in a twisted kiss, followed by the tug of her tongue as she latched onto the wound. She moved slowly, dragging up and down, savoring me, occasionally lifting her eyes to meet mine. The suction deepened into a visceral confluence.

And for one impossible moment, it almost... felt good.

The shock paralyzed me. My body went rigid, my fight folding into a hollow stillness as I stared at the crown of her head bowed over my arm.

The man stirred, then rose, his body filling the room as he moved toward us. His eyes locked on mine, confident in the way a predator knows it already owns its prey. Every muscle coiled and slid with the slow, unstoppable flow of water over stone. His penis, still slick with her juices, hung heavy as it softened. Up close, he was impossibly big in every way—towering, sinewed, built like a creature assembled from pieces never meant to fit together. If he were a character in my book, I'd say he was carved by hands that didn't fully understand anatomy, merely trying to make him as hulking and formidable as possible.

With the back of his hand, he gave his bloodied lips a perfunctory wipe. The woman must have felt him approach—not heard, for he moved silently—as she lifted her bloody, grinning face from my arm. He took the knife from her and knelt at my feet. His hands clamped around my legs with inhuman strength, pinning me like paper. My old Metallica shirt, which I slept in, rode up past my hips, leaving me bare to the cold air. I kicked, desperate, but he slid between my legs and held me down. My body stretched in both directions, helpless, the woman pressing from above, the man anchoring me below.

I screamed, thinking I knew what was coming, bracing for it—

The blade flashed—not like the woman's slow, lingering cut, but a swift, brutal strike. It tore across the tender inside of my thigh, pain spearing inward as if it struck bone. I yowled and thrashed anew.

The woman watched, aroused, eyes wide and wild, as claret dripped from her chin.

The man leaned in, and his mouth sealed over the cut on my inner thigh. He latched on and began to suck, drinking like his existence depended on it. I felt like spoiled fruit beneath his hands as he squeezed the flesh around my wound.

This isn't happening, I thought.

This wasn't real.

They couldn't be real.

They were drinking me, biting my body like wolves at a kill.

Was this what they had done to Sylvie?

The woman took the knife back and began slicing through my T-shirt, deliberately, savoring each motion. The fabric split open, exposing my bare stomach, then my breasts. She set the blade against my nipple. I jerked aside in panic.

"Shh," she whispered again. "You don't want me to cut it off by accident, do you? So beautiful. Delicate."

My nipple tightened reflexively, betraying me, as she circled it with the knife. Then she closed her lips around my puckered skin, sucking slowly, tracing the peak with her tongue, exploring, teasing, making me shiver against her touch.

I held my breath, almost forgetting the man—until he clamped down harder on my thigh. His teeth sank in deep. Pain flared anew.

Another flash of heat swept across my abdomen. She opened a thin cut on my stomach and leaned down to drink from it. As she fed, the man finally released my thigh, took the knife from her, and prepared for the next cut—on my other thigh.

They drank from me greedily, swallowing with harsh, slavering gulps that made bile crawl up the back of my throat.

They held me so tightly I could barely move, their strength crushing, inhuman. I couldn't lash out. But I could scream, and I did, until my voice cracked.

Weakness spread through me, my body failing as they drank their fill. My head jerked from side to side, powerless to resist. New cuts bloomed across my skin, some shallow, others deep enough to nick a vein.

I lost all sense of how long they had been torturing me. Minutes, maybe hours—I couldn't tell. I was stripped bare, a canvas of cuts, mired with cruor.

They had licked me all over, their mouths roaming, biting, tearing into me, never deep enough to end it, just cruel rips meant to keep me alive. The man withdrew. His hunger spent, he drifted into the shadows, leaving me limp and trembling, alone with *her*.

She crouched over me, her face shiny with sweat and sooty stains.

"Now it's just you and me, honey," she said, and I knew she was about to take her revenge for the cut I had left on her throat.

The woman reached for her scarf. She untied the knot and began to unwrap the silk.

The gape was a mortal architecture, a space nobody should survive. Yet she hovered, alive, her torso swaying over me with the fluid grace of a snake dancing to a flute.

"Look what you did," she whispered. Her voice was a damp rasp, the sound of air escaping through the wrong hole. She brushed her fingers over the edge of the wound, unsettling steam.

Then she plunged them into it.

She seized my jaw with her free hand, though I had no fight left in me. She pried my mouth open, the joints of my skull popping under the pressure. Blood-coated fingers pressed inside. I heaved, a violent gag reflex struggling against the intrusion, but she did not release. Her warmth traced my interior, the copper taste making my throat revolt. I was suffocating.

Then she eased back. For a while, she simply sat, watching me, her gaze distant, lost in a daydream.

With a subtle tremor, the knife returned, tracing my leg until it settled between my thighs. Her voice was a soft, almost tender murmur, barely audible.

"If I cut you here," she said, teasing the hood of my clit with the cold steel, "will you still shudder for me when I drink?"

My head lolled weakly to the side. How much longer could I endure this? How much longer could I be carved, licked, bitten, drained, and still live?

The woman leaned closer, her lips curved into a knowing smile.

"Let's try," she whispered, pressing harder. "Open up."

A flash of obliterating pain tore through me, the existing wounds reopening as she dug her nails into my skin, and then everything gave way.

The world tilted and dissolved, welcoming me into the blissful dark.

At last.

IV

A whimper escaped me as I fought to keep consciousness from creeping back. Life refused to depart, but I didn't want it. I wanted to be with Sylvie.

The dessicated blood married a sour, clammy sweat to my skin. The gashes, just beginning to dry, ripped open with the slightest movements. I lay there, ears straining against the sounds of the room, as I waited for what was coming next.

There was no more music. Only the soft, sinister stir of movement downstairs. Voices. Short thuds. The scrape of something heavy dragging across the floor. Were they moving furniture?

Then footsteps.

Closer. Closer.

Through lidded eyes, the woman appeared. She moved like a ghost in the half-dark, clean now, with no trace of the feast or the orgy. A flowing peignoir hung over a short lace nightgown. Her auburn hair had been brushed and curled again, silky and neat, her skin smooth as porcelain. A different scarf adorned her neck.

Cold fingers pressed against my cracked lips, holding them there to check whether I still respired.

The scent of vanilla soap and sweet, fruity shampoo was an assault. It was the scent of Sylvie after a shower. But beneath the perfume, there was a faint, grounding trace of damp soil.

"She *is* still alive!" she exclaimed, her head snapping toward the door. Her voice was high and sharp, drilling my already pounding head.

The man stood in the doorway, dressed in sweatpants, his torso bare.

"Finish her," he said in the detached, almost absurd tone of someone telling Alexa to add milk to a grocery list.

I had pleaded for death, yet hearing it pronounced like a verdict brought a terror beyond words. The craving for death was one thing; the anticipation was another. The wait was worse.

"No," the woman said with a petulant lilt. "We should keep her. For emergencies while we are here. Besides, she's so pretty, I like black hair and milky skin. Let her be for now. Let us see how long she lasts."

The man lingered in the doorway a moment longer. The hallway light cast his figure in a harsh illumination.

"Do what you want, but make sure she causes no problems, Ophelia." Then he disappeared again.

Ophelia. So the monster had a name.

She leaned closer, brushing my cheek. Her touch was gentle, yet it carried the weight of dominance. The master was letting her play with her new toy.

"You heard him," the madwoman whispered against my jugular. "You are *mine.*"

They left me chained for the entire day. No water. Sylvie's body still sprawled out like garbage. I slipped in and out of restless sleep, my dreams fractured and unsteady, forcing me to relive the horrors of the previous night.

In the stagnant heat of the room, a thin, whitish film clouded the surface of Sylvie's eyes. Decay had claimed the blush from her face, leaving her features with a waxy, translucent quality that looked more like sculpted soap than flesh. I anchored my eyes anywhere but on her.

Surrounded by this stench of human bodies and viscera, the room began to corrode. My body must have emptied while I was out, for my hair was matted with sick. And above it all was the iron: blood, blood, blood, earthy and rusted, seeping into the fabrics, the furniture, and the very bones of the house.

My chest ached with every shallow pull of air, every microscopic shift. I was still hoping that my body would simply give up. But after a few hours, the blackouts finally stalled; my mind was present once more. With nothing else to do, I began to assess the damage.

Cuts and bites of various depths mapped my skin—on my thighs, my arms, my belly, and my breasts. My nipples were chewed and raw. She hadn't harmed my genitals; at least, not that I could feel.

But the physical pain was nothing compared to the agony of remembering Sylvie was gone. She was not coming back. I would never hear her voice again. Instead, I might be forced to witness her corpse rotting—watching her lose every human feature, day after day.

At times, I forced myself to look at her, begging for the slightest twitch, but deep down, I knew she was dead.

She was covered in deep, mangled tears—nothing like the shallow gashes they had left on me. Hers were deeper, more ruthless, carved with feral hunger. Her neck was a ruinous mess, clinging to the battered remains of a head I had memorised in full to the beauty mark above bow-shaped lips and chickenpox scars on a slender nose. My Sylvie was no more.

Hours passed. I was so thirsty, driven half mad by my surroundings, that I began fading again, slipping into dreams of cool, endless water. A vast lake crowned with a roaring waterfall. In the dream, I drank, drank, drank, desperate for it to satiate me.

Then I returned to myself, and my throat was sandpaper. Every inhale scraped. Each breath felt like fire dragged through me.

The house was too far from anywhere. No one would stop by. There were no neighbors for miles. No one would wonder why Sylvie's car still sat in the driveway, untouched. No one would notice she hadn't left for work. Maybe someone would call, but not before Monday. And it was only Saturday.

I didn't know where my intruders had gone, but the house was suspiciously quiet, save for a high-pitched ringing in my ears. Every once in a while, I thought I caught a whisper, too soft and just out of reach, but when I tried to focus on it, it was gone.

Maybe they had left me here to die. Maybe they were finished with me. Maybe I could run.

But I could barely move, let alone unchain myself or break the iron of the radiator. I would wither here, slowly, forced to watch the body of my beloved spoil.

No. A stubborn instinct, buried deep in the meat of me, insisted they were still here in Whitmore—hiding, resting after the Danse Macabre they had led me through. The quiet felt wrong, the heavy moment before a new cruelty began. My end would not be quick. It would come slowly, drawn out, one slice at a time.

The woman would keep me alive only to ruin me again and again until there was nothing left. I should have stabbed her in the eye when I had the chance.

My gaze landed on the bloodied Stanley knife, just beyond my reach. I strained for it, stretching my arm until my scabs popped and fresh blood crawled down my skin. Too far. My fingertips scraped nothing but air.

Useless. Useless.

The gray day dimmed like lights in a theater, slowly and intentionally, so the darkness had time to be noticed. As the last of the daylight faded, the silence went with it. From downstairs came the sound of a door creaking open. Footsteps. I knew it was her.

Ophelia.

Her light tread climbed the stairs, lingered in the corridor, then slipped into the room. She crouched beside me, peering into my face.

"Good heavens, you're a resilient creature, aren't you?" she asked. She possessed an old-fashioned, stilted cadence, like she had stepped out of another century or was imitating the clipped tones of early sound films.

Her hands slid under my neck—so gentle, like a lover's caress. I shivered at the contact. Then, fabric brushed against my throat. Soft. Wrong. Before I could react, it tightened, pulling snug against my skin. My body stiffened, bracing for the crush of strangulation, but it never came.

Instead, the handcuffs fell away.

I turned my head, dazed, and saw a length of shimmering silk leading from my throat to her pale hand. She had leashed me with one of her scarves. Like a dog.

"C'mon," she said whimsically. "Good girl. Get up."

I pushed at the floor with trembling hands, dragging myself upward, but my legs buckled beneath me. I collapsed in a heap.

A splash of ice-cold water struck me like a slap. I choked as it rushed up my nose. My tongue lapped, desperate to catch it, but I trapped only the ghost of droplets before the house swallowed it in front of me. I tried again, frantic, licking at the film, but it disappeared faster than I could gather it. My body clawed toward life on instinct.

Ophelia tugged the leash, and I lurched forward, my chin scraping over splinters.

"You need to get rid of her before she starts to smell." She nudged Sylvie's remains with pedicured toes.

I swayed on barely-there legs and attempted to lift Sylvie into my arms with the hollow obedience carved into me by pain. Her body was so ruined I feared she would come apart in my hands, her head swinging by what looked like a single stubborn strip of skin.

I tried to lift her fully, but her weight betrayed me, slipping through my weakened grip. She fell with a meaty thud that jolted me to the core. Another strangled cry tore from me. I didn't want to hurt her, even though I understood she was far beyond pain.

I bent once more, hands slick with her blood and mine, as I clung to her with trembling fingers. The words *"sorry, sorry, sorry"* sputtered against my lips. I didn't let them out.

Sylvie's corpse sagged in my arms, the joints loose where they should have held. For some reason, her body refused the stiffening of the grave. Already, the enzymes were at work, dissolving the muscle fibers and softening the pulp until it felt grotesquely yielding. She was coming apart in my arms, her body losing cohesion as I held her.

The turned turf reeked—a sickly, raw scent like a secret meant to remain buried. Stones struck the edge of the shovel with a bone-white ring, forcing me to reach into the muck and pluck them out.

Sweat burned my eyes, stinging and blurring the world into

a haze of mud and aching muscles. My hands, raw and shuddering, grabbed the spade again. I prayed for my body to give in, to collapse and finally set my spirit free. But it refused. The flesh and bone held. My soul felt heavy, trapped stubbornly inside this useless vessel.

And there she was—Sylvie, or what was left of her. She lay at the lip of the grave, her thin fingers dangling over the edge. Every time I dared to look up, there they were, reaching for earth they could no longer feel.

Ophelia bent and touched the late blooms of a hydrangea, heavy and desperate before the winter's teeth. She caressed the corymb, and it leaned into her palm. How could she admire the flowers while I was here, digging a grave for the woman I had hoped to marry?

I didn't know how long I had been shovelling. The world had shrunk to this hole, this endless pit of earth and sorrow. My mind was a hollow void. No thoughts, no plans. Just one command: dig.

Dig. Throw the earth out. Dig again. Repeat. Repeat. Repeat.

Sylvie would be buried here, next to the gazebo she hated, the one I had wanted to save. Now it would stand over her, a crumbling monument to what had been lost forever.

My mind drifted. I was eleven. My stepdad's car had struck my dog, Saddy, leaving her whimpering and barely alive. He was furious, yelling at me even though the car was unharmed. He blamed me for letting her run loose. She lay there suffering, and there was nothing I could do but hold her, my heart pounding in helpless despair. He refused to take her to the vet. Instead, he left for work, the slam of the door an exclamation mark on the matter.

The house was empty, except for Saddy and me. My mother was on a night shift, and by the time she returned, Saddy was gone. Mother told me to get her out of the house before my stepdad came home. I had to drag her body into the woods, fighting the unwilling forest floor as I dug. I cried until the salt burned my throat. The grave came out so shallow. A few days later, wild animals worked Saddy back to the surface. The stench of death announced her desecration long before I approached.

"Enough." A voice fell on me from above.

I drifted slowly from the reverie, the night pressing in. The horror of the present flooded my fevered brain.

God? It's me. I never believed, but look at me now. Reach into this pit and pull me out. Save me.

But there was never a God.

Ophelia kicked Sylvie's body. My beloved's hand jerked lifelessly in response. I flinched, aghast at the lack of sensitivity.

One final shove sent Sylvie into the pit. The impact knocked me off my feet. I fell on top of her, struck by her chill. Sylvie had always been warm, even under the thinnest blankets—the reason she hated cuddling in bed. I had been the one shivering nonstop, my limbs frozen. Now I burned. I was drenched in sweat; hatred and fury coursing through me.

"Get up," the woman ordered. "Get out."

I wanted to resist, to wrench free, but I could not. It was not hypnosis—only exhaustion. Bone-deep, absolute weariness. My body moved before my mind could gather its will, obeying the silent, relentless command.

I stood, staring down at Sylvie's crumpled form, half-swallowed by night. When my mind finally caught up, it gave in —not from fear but from complete depletion, too spent to struggle, too hollow to argue. Inside, I was dead. I wanted it all to end, yet some stubborn flicker of life remained, clinging and dragging out the torment a little longer.

But the work was not done. The earth gaped with black teeth, the broken body of the woman I loved clutched within its jaw.

I couldn't stop watching as Sylvie slowly disappeared, and something in me died with her.

The woman I loved was gone, and I was the one burying her.

I was alone with my grief. Alone with the finality of death—all while the monster who'd brought it upon us stood there, admiring the late blooms.

V

The lunatic woman returned me to the room where Sylvie had died. She chained me to the radiator and left me there, trapped in the prison of my own mind. Except for the few drops I managed to gather from the floor, I had not had any water. My consciousness began to swim. Daylight seeped through the curtained window like a cruel mercy, the world beyond my reach.

Here, time was senescing with me.

Thankfully, I didn't have long.

The thin fabric around my throat, the one the woman had forgotten to remove, felt unbearably heavy. I no longer had the strength to move or pull it away. Every swallow felt like glass wool.

Where had they gotten the handcuffs? They did this often, didn't they? Prepared to invade houses like mine. It was no coincidence they came here. They had chosen this place because it was isolated, and because they could watch us without anyone noticing. So I sat there, at the bottom of the world, chasing the same thoughts in circles. Each time they returned, they were different, warped and distorted, until I could trust them no longer. Until I couldn't trust myself.

Sometimes I heard whispers in the walls, or the scrape of bone across the floor, though nothing moved.

Sometimes I thought I had never been anywhere but here, chained in this stinking pit.

None of my memories felt real. Not the sun. Not the house. I couldn't remember my own name. Even Sylvie, her gentle image, the only thing I kept clinging to, seemed like a mirage.

Maybe I had imagined it all.

The door swung open, and stark light from the hall stabbed my eyes like hot coals. Every part of my body ached, but it was a dull kind of pain, muted by exhaustion and submission. The madwoman came into the room barefoot. Her gown was thin, gliding like a shadow with the iridescence of a butterfly's wing. She drifted rather than walked. Unnatural. Had she come to finish me?

"Hey there, sunshine." Her voice was mellifluous, poison coated in honey. She lowered herself beside me. "I brought you something."

At first, I thought it was a plastic ball, round and smooth. It rolled toward me soundlessly, coming to a halt in the dead space between us.

I didn't move. Every muscle drew tight as I watched her, waiting for the sudden lunge.

"It's for you."

A tangerine.

I stayed curled in on myself, knees drawn to my chest, trying to shrink small enough to disappear. It looked obscene, too bright and vibrant.

She nudged it closer with the back of her hand.

Against my will, I yearned forward for the fruit. In my mind,

I could already feel the spray of its sharp, citric oil between my teeth; the way the flesh would burst against my tongue like a haemorrhage. But it lived only in my mind.

It was too far. The chain reached its end, the iron snapping taut with a dull, final note before I gained even an inch.

Hatred burned through the fog in my head. This woman had taken everything. And now she stood over me, mocking what little remained of my humanity. With the last of my strength, I gripped the radiator behind my back and twisted, trying to swing my legs toward her, to hurt her somehow, even a little.

But she was faster.

Her hand caught the end of the scarf and yanked. The knot tightened at once. A sharp jerk crushed my windpipe, and the world shrank to that single point of pressure at my throat.

Then released.

My body collapsed back against the chain, shaking. For several long seconds, the air refused to come.

She was on me before I could return to my senses. Faster, stronger, and impossibly heavy for her thin frame. Her knees pinned my ribs, squeezing the air from my lungs until the world blurred. One hand pressed my wrist flat against the floor, pinning me to the cold grain. The other held the tangerine.

I stilled.

"You will behave now," she ordered coolly. Still straddling me, she began to peel the skin. Each strip of rind tore away with a faint snap. The scent burst into the room, severe and sugary, mingling with the sour reek of my own exhaustion and the stench of waste soaked into the rug. My mouth flooded with saliva, and my stomach twisted so violently I almost retched.

The fruit sagged in her hand. It was mottled, beginning to spot the way fruit does when it starts to turn. Sylvie had bought them days earlier, after her dentist scolded her for not getting enough Vitamin C. A bag of bright little suns had sat in the bowl on the kitchen counter; I hadn't touched them. Neither had she.

Now, one had followed me here, half-spoiled, clinging to the last of its firmness the way my body clung to life against my mind's will.

She broke off a slice and pressed it against my lips—not hard, but insistent. I turned my head, but her hand followed, patient and unrelenting.

"Open," she cooed.

Instinct betrayed me.

Tart syrup awoke my senses. It was not what I had imagined; there was nothing refreshing in it. First came a fleeting sweetness, then a deep bitterness, and finally a strange metallic edge, as though the fruit had begun to ferment from the inside out. She watched me the way a mother might watch a child swallow medicine. I chewed slowly, never looking away from her.

When I forced the piece down, she gave a small, satisfied smile and began to peel another. Her hands moved almost reverently.

She fed me one slice, then another. I wanted to stop, to retch, to pull away from her eyes, unblinking and too intent, but I ate because she willed it.

When the fruit was gone, I watched her and waited for the next cruelty, the next game. She shifted her weight, and the pressure holding me down eased.

"Get up, pup. Let's go."

She took my hands. They no longer felt or looked like my own. They were obscene—a stranger's meat, bruised and sticky with blood. In comparison, Ophelia's were cool and smooth, untouched by the filth and stench of me. Not a single muscle in her face flinched. I wondered what it felt like to be so composed.

With an irresistible insistence, she coaxed me up. My hands remained trapped in hers as she led the way. Step by step, we climbed into the dark of the third floor. The rooms there were empty and unfurnished. Bare walls, bare floors, nothing but the echo of our steps.

Candles burned everywhere. My eyes watered at once, stung by the smoke and aggressive light. I couldn't tell how much time had passed. Like me, day and night had lost their meaning.

I blinked through the glare, straining for a glimpse of the outside, some sign that the world still existed.

The windows stopped me cold.

Each one had been covered with plywood and reinforced with thick planks. Nails bit through beams softened by decades of moisture. The boards crossed over the glass in tight lines.

Was this done while I was under? The sheer effort of it, to what end? Did they really think I'd leap from the third floor? Or did they just want to make sure I forgot the world existed?

Inside, there was only the house, closed in on itself, its timber creaking softly. The air felt close and stale; Whitmore had drawn a lid over itself, keeping me inside.

The bed, once stark, had been transformed. The mattress was a century-old ruin Sylvie and I had meant to throw away, but now it was draped in a deep-red sheet. Pillows sat atop the headboard—stolen from the couch downstairs. There was no duvet.

From the bedposts, chains hung in wait. Fresh iron, prepared for the sole purpose of holding me.

But Ophelia did not steer me to the bed. Not yet.

Instead, she led me to the bathroom. Unlike the rest of the house, this room was shrouded in a darkness so thick it felt sluggish. A candle struggled near the mirror. No curtain shielded the tub, and no clutter broke the cold expanse of the counters. A lone dressing table stood against the far wall, a small stool tucked beneath the surface. On top, next to the candle, rested a single round object, its wood worn smooth by the passage of years. An antique hairbrush. The handle was a silver-shadowed work of art, thick and intricate, with vines that coiled around the grip. The bristles were stiff, set into an ivory handle.

The woman left me standing there, still dazed, and turned on the water. The tub began to fill. Steam slowly cushioned the cold air. When she looked back at me, her expression was calm.

"Let's go, pup. You can brush my hair."

She sat before the glass, very still, her hair falling over her shoulders like molten lava. Her face carried a strange, delicate youth, almost doll-like, yet her eyes remained empty and watchful.

She placed the polished bone in my hand.

The brush did not belong to me. It wasn't Sylvie's either. Though it was certainly something she would have loved to own. She would have used it, too; she was the kind of person who advocated for using the fine china every day, never locking things away just to preserve them. She loved beautiful things, but never as museum pieces meant to sit untouched on a shelf. She wanted to demonstrate extravagance, even if there was no one to show off to.

She told me once how her mother would keep gifts wrapped because the paper was too beautiful to tear. That was why Sylvie never wrapped anything for her. When her mother died, and we were cleaning out her house, I saw the truth of it myself: dozens of boxes, the paper old and yellowed, thick with decades of dust. She hadn't cared for the things inside; she only cared for the getting, the hoarding.

Sylvie was the opposite.

"Some things are made beautiful to be destroyed," she used to say as she wrapped Christmas presents, paper folding obediently beneath her soft touch. "Their beauty lives in how quickly they pass."

She said it lightly, almost teasingly, but those words had once soothed the quiet shame I carried from childhood, the belief that I ruined every good thing placed in my hands. She made me tear the delicate wrapping and laugh about it.

Sylvie.

Her hair was now clotted with soil. Worms threading through the strands. There was no use for beautiful things anymore.

Ophelia relaxed into my strokes, her head tilting back slightly as she closed her eyes.

And then, a snag. At the very root of her hair, a tiny piece of dirt fisted a lock. It looked wrong, a blemish on a thing so clean. I wondered where it had come from, along with that faint scent of stale mud. After all, she hadn't been digging graves; that was a labor assigned to me.

I tried catching it with the brush, but her hair was so thick and heavy that the bristles simply glided over it. Slipping into a narrow, airless hyperfocus, I was about to reach in when she shifted uncomfortably and looked straight at me.

"No, not like this."

She took the brush and, with a smooth caress, demonstrated exactly how she wanted it done. The motion was slow, sensual even, coaxing a purr from her once-open throat. Then she placed the brush back in my palm, folding my fingers around it one by one as she guided me through the motion.

As she released me, her touch lingered over her trauma, now an angry pink scar. Only now did I realize she wasn't wearing a scarf to hide the wound. Just her necklace, which, upon closer look, appeared like a little vial on a chain.

I tried to search for the passage of time. Had it been a day? Two? It couldn't have been more than three. But the mark on her throat looked at least a week old. My own lacerations were still fresh, weeping, and they were not nearly as deep as hers.

She caught my gaze in the mirror. "See what you did."

I was unable to look away. I had done that. My only regret was that it had not killed her.

"I should make you pay for it," she continued, her voice soft as ash. "Maybe I will give you scars of your own."

But she already had. Mine were the kind that would never heal. I caught a glimpse of my reflection. My black hair was a matted mess, glued together with ichor. I didn't recognize myself, and yet, the sight didn't terrify me as it should. My reflection was just as much of a stranger as the one before me. I did exactly as Ophelia had demonstrated, massaging her hair from scalp to tip. The longer I worked, the less natural she seemed. Her beauty had an unsettling quality. It was too precise, too still, like a figure that almost looked human but was not quite.

She caught my gaze in the mirror again, and I lowered my eyes, unwilling to feel that lethal stare pressing into me.

Then, she grabbed my arm.

The brush struck the floor and bounced into the void beneath the vanity. She studied me in the steamy glass, searching for something I could not name.

At first, I didn't understand what she meant to do.

Then her incisors flashed.

Soft lips brushed my wrist. Teeth followed, tearing open the deep cut there once more. I gasped and tried to pull away, but her grip held fast. She fed as if it were the simplest thing in the world.

I wanted to scream, but the act caught like a noose. The way she sucked and licked, vicing my arm, was close to erotic.

A warmth pooled between my legs.

It was wrong. I wasn't supposed to feel this way.

I jerked back, but since I hadn't expected her to actually let go, the sudden lack of resistance sent me tumbling. I reeled from the force of my own movement and fell hard onto the splintered floorboards.

"I think the bathtub is full," she said, nonchalantly, and rose from the chair with grace.

Holding my wrist against my chest, I pushed myself up and followed her. I moved without protest—obedient, like the animal she was training me to become.

The bathtub was not just full; it had begun to overflow. Water cascaded over the enamel rim in a steady sheet. *The floor is ruined. We'll never be able to sell the house*—a delayed, useless thought, a ghost of my past life.

She did not hurry to turn the tap off. Her movements remained languid. "Get in."

She spoke with the same calm authority I once used with Saddy when it was time to wash her. She loved the water when it was a river or a lake, but the bathtub filled her with dread. Even so, she never snapped or tried to bolt. She simply endured it while I worked the soap through her fur, standing there, drenched and miserable.

I used to believe she did it because she loved me. That she remained still because she knew what would happen if she ran: my stepdad would beat me.

I moved toward the tub, but Ophelia skimmed my chest, halting me with that same unbearable tenderness.

"Undress first, silly."

I was wearing the same T-shirt I'd had on the night they arrived, now gaping down the middle where she'd cut through it. The fabric had dried into my cuts, fusing with the scabs. It would hurt to remove. Still, I gripped the hem and pulled, before sinking into the tub.

The water was warmer than I expected. Goosebumps rose on skin that no longer felt my own. Every cut burned on contact. Blood loosened from the reopened wound and unraveled into the water in thin, fading ribbons. Ophelia settled on the bath's edge, poised as a cat, and watched me wash. I wondered, fleetingly, if she wanted to do it for me.

The sensation cleared my head slightly, though my thoughts still swam, dulled by hunger. That pathetic, moribund tangerine had only scraped at my insides. I needed food. I needed to get away.

A sudden strength, akin to terminal clarity, flooded my veins. Simply running away was no longer enough. I needed her blood in the dirt.

Ophelia was strong; there was no overpowering her. Not yet. I had to wait. I had to endure. I would wait until she was certain I was broken, drained of every ounce of resistance. Then, I would turn and strike.

She took a wet cloth to my skin and began scrubbing away the layers of dirt and grime.

"I don't want to use soap," she said. "I like your natural scent. It's so . . ." She leaned in, inhaling me until her eyes rolled back. ". . . euphoric. You smell like sex and magnolias and railroad tracks on a hot day."

Soon after, she rose and left, only to return seconds later with a nightgown the pallor of pale sick. Like the other robes Ophelia donned, this garment was utterly unfamiliar. Did she travel with a wardrobe of luxury nightwear?

"Here." She held the piece open for me, shrugging it up over my damp shoulders. The fabric dropped and stuck to my knees, a slit rising to mid-thigh. I thought I saw Ophelia's stare linger there.

"Look." She turned me toward the mirror. The piece was like gossamer, revealing the sharpness of a body I no longer knew. It was an exposure worse than simple nakedness. A kind meant to tease. It hid nothing; not the keen peaks of my nipples nor the soot-black curls of my pubic hair.

I grimaced.

Ophelia, however, seemed delighted.

"This color is darling on you!" she chirped, trailing a fingernail along my collarbone. "I am going to call you Agatha, for you are brave." She stepped back, hands folded under her chin, appraising me with the careful scrutiny of someone inspecting art.

"Gunnar!" she called. And just like that, the second monster had a name.

Half a minute later, a shadow filled the doorway, banishing the air with its formidable presence. Pressure pressed across the ridge of my nose, as if Gunnar himself were touching me.

It was the first time I truly saw him. I could not guess his age —thirty, forty, fifty? Impossible to tell. His face looked like a mask, only his dark eyes alive beneath it.

He looked at me, then at her.

"This is Agatha." Ophelia spun me, and I felt like cattle being shown at auction.

"Ophelia." Her name was a clap of thunder from his lips.

She jumped, words tumbling like a child begging a parent before refusal could come.

"She's so resilient! She can help us clean and feed! And you're always sitting with your bones. I have no one to keep me company. Please?"

He glanced at me again, and I met his eyes, holding them like a prayer. It was clear he was in charge. It was clear he did not want me alive. One shift of expression could have been my death sentence. And suddenly, I wanted to live, to fight, to see the end of them.

"Make sure it's not like the last time," he said, before stomping away.

She nodded and turned to me, teeth bared in a wide grin. I could not help but wonder what had happened the last time, but I said nothing.

Ophelia seated me at the vanity and retrieved the brush. Her hands tangled like curses through my hair. She tried to be gentle, but it still pulled, and I fought not to wince. I would not give her the satisfaction of my pain. I kept my head straight, meeting my reflection in the mirror.

Oh, how I wanted my hatred to spill out and suffocate her.

The decor was somewhere between Victorian, Fifty Shades and Slaughterhouse. In the guest room, Ophelia had cloaked the bed in lace, bolted thick chains to the frame, plumped chintzy cushions, and banished sunlight from ever entering. Still, it was a step up from the bloodied bedroom and the imprint of Sylvie's corpse. During the day, while she and Gunnar were away or sleeping, I remained in shackles. Whitmore, for all intents and purposes, was out of bounds. I couldn't even use the bathroom.

I lay there for hours staring into the black and thinking that perhaps this was what death felt like. Floating in emptiness. But then the old mattress would creak beneath me, and I would remember that I was not so lucky as to die immediately, like Sylvie.

Sylvie. I cried so much thinking of her. I could almost feel her body decomposing out there. Slowly, she was erasing herself from my mind. One night, I struggled to recall if her birthmark sat upon her right cheek or her chin; the next, the exact shade of her hair slipped away. The faces of the people I once knew were deliquescing, blurring into a single, featureless mass.

But I needed her. The memory was the final thread tethering me to the life I'd lost. As long as she lived in my mind, she wasn't fully gone.

Later that day, when I struggled to recall her, I twisted in my bindings, hauling the mattress corner up until my hand could reach the bed frame. Hours passed as I carved her name into the wood. My nails sloughed from their beds, bleeding, but I kept on until the letters were gouged deep: S-Y-L-V-I-E.

I stared at my work. The word looked foreign—seized symbols, like hieroglyphs that were supposed to mean something, but I could no longer comprehend.

When night came, I was usually woken by the music starting again, or by the creak of the bedroom door and the small flame of the candle Ophelia carried in her hand. For some reason, she disliked electric light, and whenever I was with her, we were surrounded by candles.

Where did she find so many? Did she buy them? Steal them? Sylvie and I had only ever kept emergency lamps, never candles, for fear of burning down the house.

We fell into a kind of ritual where she'd wash me, brush my hair, and dress me in translucent fabrics. Then she would place the brush in my hand and turn her back, ready to be indulged. I would brush her hair in long strokes while she watched herself in the mirror, daring to catch me watching, too. And then, she would stand skyclad before the wardrobe, gesturing for me to help her choose what to wear. Dress after dress embraced and then collapsed from her lithe figure. Neither Sylvie nor I had ever owned such pieces. Ophelia must have brought them with her. And what a curation she had! There were weightless peignoirs and short gowns. Some were frothing with ruffles and lace; others were plain silk that clung to her body like a second skin.

I did not speak. I did what she wanted.

I was starving.

The food in the house was fermenting. Fruit collapsed into itself. Bread stiffened. I didn't know what they ate besides my blood, but it was clearly not what I did. Ophelia brought me whatever she could find. Yeasty tangerines. Bananas gone black. One day, a can of cold beans. Another day, oats mixed with water. Once she brought me a jar of jam. It was old, but I dug into it. Strawberry jelly smeared over my hands and cheeks until I resembled a rabid animal.

The sugar shocked my system. My taste had dulled from hunger, and the sweetness hurt. Soon, the tremors started, and my stomach twisted until I thought I would vomit.

I drank as much water as I could. It did not help. Fatigue clung to me. I lost weight, I lost muscle, and I felt oddly arthritic, wincing at the throb of joints and grinding bones, but that, by some miracle, was alleviating with every passing day.

Despite my skeletal likeness, my body healed its wounds. Beneath the bathwater, pallid skin seemed to restore, renewed like sand smoothed by ocean surf.

Though my muscles had atrophied, I kept hauling the mattress up to stare at her name until it was etched into my retina, into the core of my brain.

SYLVIE.

SYLVIE.

SYLVIE.

The night before, when Ophelia had forced me to bathe, I'd drunk until I was bloated, and now the pressure in my bladder was getting more urgent by the minute. I was so weak. I tried to heave my hips, to lift myself from the bedding, but my body foundered. My stamina betrayed me, and I felt the warmth of urine trickling out, soaking through Ophelia's gown and into the mattress.

A strange shame washed over me, and I wept from it. My

own body was failing, leaking like a cracked jar. Would Ophelia be angry? Had she not expected this, keeping me chained for twenty hours at a time?

I must have drifted still in the puddle of my own piss, for I awoke to her soft voice calling me. "Oh no, honey, did you soil yourself? I'm so sorry. Let's get you cleaned up." She unfastened the locks on my wrists and ankles.

Heavy, I limped toward the bathroom. Behind me, Ophelia let out a sharp breath. I turned to see the mattress half-dragged from the frame. She was staring at the marks I'd left—at Sylvie's name—before turning her hard eyes toward me.

"What is this? Did you do this?"

She threw the mattress to the floor and strode to me, forcing my raw, torn fingertips toward my face. "Is this how you're repaying me? Am I not enough for you? Do I not treat you well? Well, let's see what else I can do for you!"

She dragged me by the wrist into the bathroom, and there, she wrenched the tap open. The water was so hot that the steam clouded the mirror in seconds. She ripped the silk gown from my back, leaving me shivering and bare before shoving me toward the filling tub.

I hesitated. The heat came off the surface in a thick wave. It was too hot.

"Get in!" she ordered.

I stepped inside. My skin pulled tight, stinging against the heat. Only then did she touch the dial, letting the cold water break the scald. She pushed me down into the basin, the water creeping up my back. Then she pressed her hand into the center of my chest, pinning me to the bottom.

The water rose. I tried to pull my head up when it hit my ears, but she held firm.

I looked at her, my heart thumping. She wasn't drowning me, was she?

But she didn't let go. The water covered my mouth, then my nose. I managed one deep, panicked breath before I was under.

The roar of the faucet smoothed out into a deep hum as water pressed into my ear canals. It was almost peaceful, a white noise that wrapped around my head and cut me off from Ophelia and the horror of being hers.

But within that hum, there were voices.

It sounded like a distant crowd, murmurs layered on top of one another. I couldn't catch a single word, but the cadence was there, the rise and fall of many people speaking at once. *To me?*

I opened my eyes. Through the shifting surge of water, I saw Ophelia's face, rippled now. But there was no one else in the bathroom with us.

The air in my lungs began to burn, demanding release. I held it until my chest ached . . . and then let it go in a frantic burst of bubbles.

She hauled me out at once.

The air hit me like a fist.

"See what you made me do?" Her voice was level again, not even a trace of anger. She reached for the shampoo bottle behind her and squeezed the contents into her palm.

Ophelia lathered me, massaging my scalp and the nape of my neck. Her hands were much firmer than before, more meticulous. More insistent. I stiffened when she traced the line of my collarbone, coming to kneel at the edge of the tub. She slid her hand into the water. Ripples fanned out, breaking the reflection of the candlelight against the tiles. Her fingers moved with tenderness. She traced the map of healing scars along my ribs, her touch light as a moth's wing, before her hand drifted lower.

My muscles tensed.

What was she doing now?

"Shhh," she whispered into my ear, her other hand tracing the column of my neck.

I wanted to flinch, to recoil, but she gripped my hair and pulled my head back.

"I'm sorry, Agatha. I'll make it up to you."

Her hand slipped between my legs, moving through the wiry curls until she finally found me. I remembered that first night, the sensation of the blade she had pressed against my core. Now, my lower belly grew heavy with anticipation. A physical betrayal.

I wondered how my body could react this way. To the woman who killed Sylvie.

She moved her fingers with a fluency stripped of any hurry. She forced my legs open the moment I tried to close them. I tried to pretend nothing was happening, but slowly, the animal gave in. My hips started rolling against my will, moving to the rhythm of her doing, rubbing harder. She pinned me down with one palm, offering only a teasing friction where my flesh was screaming for more.

I squeaked, a broken sound swallowed by the slapping of the water. I squeezed my eyes shut, trying to find the version of myself that was still mourning Sylvie. But the dark behind my lids was no longer empty. It was filled with the heat of Ophelia's prying fingers.

She leaned in, her lips grazing the shell of my ear. Again and again, she stroked and pushed, stroked and pushed. My insides coiled, knotting around her strokes, painting ancient symbols on my core. I detested myself for fisting the tub, for dropping my head and moaning, but something primal had been woken and now required satisfaction. My centre tightened until it snapped—and then, a white-hot surge that made my toes curl against the enamel. My back arched, and I let out a low, fractured whimper.

It was over in a heartbeat, leaving me vacant and shivering. Every sensation turned unbearable, even the water against my skin felt like too much.

Ophelia withdrew her hand and stood up, watching as the tremors settled around my thighs. A kiss landed on my temple.

"Wasn't it nice?"

When I returned to bed, the mattress was back on the frame and flipped. Beneath it, my scribbles were gone. A layer of wood had been planed away, leaving only the reminder of something that used to be there.

Every few days, they came with a razor.

Ophelia made two cuts, always in the same place, on my right thigh, opening the skin just above the scars that had nearly healed. One for her. One for him. Then they drank from me.

I didn't fight. I lay still and stared at the ceiling while they fed.

Sometimes I thought I heard voices, like when Ophelia tried to drown me. Soft whispers from beyond the walls, as if someone else were moving through the house. I couldn't discern the language, nor whether they were human at all. Whether they were a fever-induced bloom of the mind or a haunting of Whitmore, remained unclear. But I found their soft murmurs soothing whenever Gunnar and Ophelia fed on me.

They never took too much. Just enough to leave me lightheaded.

Afterward, Gunnar sometimes left the room, leaving me alone with Ophelia. She never held back. She forced my hands and my mouth until she took her pleasure, then worked my body until I was sweating and shivering, pleading for release in every sense of the word.

Other nights, they both stayed.

And fucked.

A lot.

I didn't look, yet even with my back turned, I felt them. The old bed creaked; the mattress dipped and rocked beneath their weight. The room filled with the sound of it. The smell of it. Ophelia would moan, working on him with a frenetic oscillation.

Sometimes, without meaning to, I caught her looking at me while she was on him. Her mouth would fall open, panting and loose, pupils drawn tight and small, as someone lost deep inside a fever. Now and then, her lidded sight would lock on mine, as if she wanted to see whether I was still there, still listening.

I thought about how rarely Sylvie and I had touched each other in the past year. Once a month, if I was lucky. In the final months, there had been nothing at all.

Ophelia gasped, pulling me out of my thoughts, and I knew he had entered her. She lay on her back. At some point, her hand shot out and tangled in my hair, pulling hard. Whether she meant to or not, she held on as she came. I stayed rigid while her grip burned my roots, forcing me to brace against the shaking of her body.

But this wasn't over. As soon as she opened her eyes again, she pressed a firm palm into Gunnar's bare chest, stopping him from finding his own release.

"I want to watch you and her," she purred.

Everything inside me locked. I hadn't been with a man since college, and even then, it had felt empty and mechanical.

They shifted on the bed. Gunnar seized my legs and forced them apart. The mattress dipped as he moved closer, his body pressing against mine. Like Ophelia, he wore a small vial around his neck, and now it swung low, brushing my forehead with its sway. I flinched, bracing for the tear. I had seen his size. I knew it would not be gentle.

With Ophelia, the violation had been different. She had turned it into something twisted and intimate, a slow invasion that coaxed pleasure out of my body whether I wanted it or not.

But *this. . . This* was meant to hurt.

Ophelia wanted to watch me break. She wanted the kind of pain she could not give me herself.

My jaw clenched so hard I thought my teeth might crack. I lay there rigid, hollow, trying to empty myself of feeling. I told myself I was already gone. Already dead.

But not dead enough.

He gathered himself in his palm. When he finally entered me, my body yielded without resistance, opening around him with a disgusting softness that reminded me of food shedding its shape. Maybe I'd expended the last of my strength with Ophelia to resist now. Maybe I secretly craved the idea of more, of release, of losing myself. There was no fight left in me. I was simply open for him to take, take, take.

His body bore down on me and filled me, but it was his mind that pressed deeper, crowding the space inside my skull like a hand pushing through water to seize my soul. I felt unmoored under his gaze. He peered deep, touching the insides of my mind. Perhaps he possessed a power akin to a snake's, stilling his prey so it wouldn't flee, turning my body into a pliable material for his own pleasure. It was easier to blame this; to believe it wasn't me, but a force I never possessed the power to resist.

And in that knowledge, I found a small comfort. If my body were no longer mine, then what happened to it didn't have to be mine either.

He gripped my tresses and wrenched my head back, driving into me with more force. I searched for pain. For pleasure. For something I could cling to. There was nothing. Only the slick slap of flesh. The dull rhythm of his body working into mine. The pressure of being filled again and again.

My body moved with him while my mind slipped further away, sinking into an incarnadine tangle of blood, death, and stolen pleasure.

Perhaps I hadn't been a good partner to Sylvie.

Perhaps she had been right to look for a way out.

I had seen it in her. I knew what she wanted.

And I would not let her go.

I would not.

Yet she still found a way to leave me.

By dying.

By the hands of the man forcing himself into me now, while my body opened for him without protest.

A cold hand hooked beneath my chin and tilted my head.

Ophelia.

Her nails sank into my cheek, forcing me to fall into the black oceans of her eyes. She began to trace my hair, her touch deceptively light until the fingers suddenly coiled and tightened. She gripped the strands with the same bruising force Gunnar used.

Her free hand drifted lower, disappearing between her thighs where she forged a circular motion—slow at first, then sharpening in pace as she adjusted to herself. She pressed into the sheet, her hips rolling in perfect reciprocity with Gunnar's thrusts.

She kept a steady stare as her pleasure built, a faint pink rising in her cheeks—the same flush that had marked her skin when she was with him.

Gunnar drove deeper, relentless.

Ophelia rode herself faster, freer. A tremor ran across her face, a subtle twitch beneath the skin. Her lashes fluttered, her eyes finally breaking contact with mine. Gunnar growled low in his throat. The sound reverberated through the bedframe. His body pressed tight against mine, thrusting hard before spilling hot inside me.

Beside us, Ophelia broke. Her hand pressed harder between her thighs, her hips jerking with each motion. A raw, ragged sound tore loose as her body convulsed, then relaxed, trembling uncontrollably next to mine.

I lay rigid beneath them, my hair tangled in their hands, the warmth they'd stolen from me now cooling across my skin. I was empty and full all at once, every nerve raw and alight, my body no longer my own. But I hadn't finished. And there was a small relief in that. It meant that even now, in their full possession, there was a part of my mind they couldn't touch.

And so it started. They drew me in regularly, pulling me from the edges of the bed into the heat of it. I was no longer a silent observer, no longer merely a tool in their fantasy of being watched.

Gunnar didn't want me in any human sense. To me, it seemed he simply indulged his companion's whims. He was the strength of their murderous pair, yet he chose his battles, offering his power to her willingly. And though there was no rational explanation, I knew in my mind that he drew no more pleasure from me than he did from her. I was just meat—not even the piece he would have chosen.

An unspoken understanding settled between us: I didn't resist him when he drank from me or took my body, and he did nothing extra to hurt me.

Sex with men had never offered me a sense of wholeness. It always reduced me to a vessel, a tool for a single purpose. As a woman, I was a space to be used, a place where they could lay their weight and find relief. Like a bathroom. I meant only to serve their desire, never my own.

And now, with him, the horror was no longer in the anticipation of pain, but in its absence. My body accepted him, just as it accepted Ophelia's touch, growing willing and ready the longer it endured. I couldn't tell if the heat in my skin was a response to their pleasure or some vitiated contamination, a parasite rooted deep in my gut, thriving against my will.

I felt obscene.

Ophelia always stayed close. Sometimes she perched on the edge of the bed, sometimes in the chair beside it, watching. Other times, she guided my hand across her body, into her wetness, using me like any other object in the room, another instrument of her pleasure. In every way that mattered, she and Gunnar were alike.

Their hunger for blood was expanding. They drained me almost every night. Ophelia always stepped in before Gunnar took too much. Her hand closed around his wrist and held him back. The act suggested she was saving me for something else. Even with that restraint, my body began to unravel.

Two weeks passed. Maybe three. I no longer trusted myself to know.

Days—or rather nights, for I no longer stirred while the sun was up—blurred together into one endless dark. I clung to Sylvie in my mind, summoning her face as it had been. At first, it came easily: her faded blue eyes, sharp cheekbones, that crooked smile, the subtle lift of her right eyebrow, the little asymmetries I loved.

But with each passing night, the edges frayed. The lines of her face softened, then dissolved. Her voice grew faint, blending into the other whispers I had been hearing through the walls.

It felt like watching her die a second time—this time slowly, inside my own head.

On some nights, I would wake and wait for Ophelia to come upstairs to initiate our routine, but she did not always come. I knew she was in the house because her agitated voice would rise against Gunnar.

Their fights were nothing like those I once had with Sylvie. With her, there had been doors slammed hard enough to rattle walls. There was always an insufferable punishment of silence. I would try to soothe her, telling her we could fix things, while she admitted she was no longer sure she wanted me at all. I had always convinced her it would get better.

Gunnar and Ophelia fought differently. I had overheard enough to know she resented the time he spent alone in the room beside mine, the one filled with stifled whispers. Gunnar never raised his voice. Only Ophelia. Her vocals carried with the wounded pitch of a spoiled child.

Gunnar looked at me more often now, pinning me with his gaze while he used my body. Perhaps he wondered if I was the reason Ophelia was spinning out of control. The attention was unsettling, but it also brought a strange comfort. For a moment,

I felt less snubbed and more like something with shape. A person, perhaps.

Ophelia clung to me with a kind of aching urgency. She moved against my body to find her own release, using me until she broke, and afterward, she held me close, as though we were lovers.

The scar on her neck had vanished completely now. And perhaps she had forgiven me.

Or perhaps she was smoothing me out before she broke me fully.

When I woke, it was not to noise but to a tense quiet.

I had learned to tell their movements apart even with my eyes closed. Gunnar never entered this room without Ophelia, yet I often heard him climb to the third floor and retreat into the room beside mine.

"She's not enough! We either finish her or you find someone else!"

Gunnar's voice carried through the stairwell, the steps groaning beneath his weight.

Everything inside me froze. Was he speaking about ending me? Now? No. No.

The door opened. My body stiffened, bracing for a fight, but it was not him. Ophelia stood there with a candle, the flame trembling in the draft. Another door slammed somewhere nearby. Gunnar had gone to his room. I couldn't help but wonder what was in there.

Ophelia sometimes mentioned it with open scorn. He spent too much time there, she said, whispering to the dead. I never asked what she meant. I no longer had the strength to form the words, let alone search for answers. I finally took the world, however ugly and grotesque, for what it was without questioning it. I stopped trying to reshape it, or bend it to my will for I no longer had a will.

"I'm just so lonely, Agatha," Ophelia said softly. "I'm so glad you're here with me. You have no idea how long I've been wanting a friend."

I kept thinking about what Gunnar had said earlier. *Not like the last time.* Whatever had happened before, it had not ended well.

When she removed the shackles and motioned for me to follow, I obeyed. I always obeyed. My body trailed after her as though pulled by a thread.

"I need your help, darling." Ophelia led me to the master bedroom.

I startled at the threshold. The room was so unwelcoming. Who would ever want to live here? It was choked with old, mismatched furniture that didn't belong together. The wallpaper was so dark it swallowed what little light made it inside. No couple sharing this space would ever be happy.

Now, dust lay thick along the baseboards. The floor bore old stains I didn't want to identify. The mattress was marked with stiff, darkened streaks. Even the radiator where she had chained me carried discoloration along the metal, like rust that had never been cleaned away.

This was the kind of room you would see in a true crime documentary, a place that made no effort to conceal what had happened there. A murder room.

She pointed to a bucket of cloudy, soapy water and a brush in the corner.

"If you could try cleaning up a bit, you would be of so much help." It was spoken so playfully, but I had come to learn the directness lurking beneath. An order, not an option.

Something caught my eye beneath the headboard. A small object, dull in the weak light. The Stanley knife.

My gaze fixed on it and would not move.

It would not kill her. Of course not. But if she left me here long enough, I could reach it. I could end it. I could leave on my own terms.

My chest ached with the thought. And more terrifyingly, I wondered if I actually wanted it to end.

Above me lay the room where Gunnar spent so many hours. His steps traveled through the beams, each one a reminder of how close they were. How little distance separated me from them.

By the time I forced my eyes away from the knife, Ophelia had returned.

She crouched and lifted it between two fingers.

"You won't be needing that," she said. Her smile hitched higher. Then she left and locked the door.

I dipped the brush into the bucket and began to scrub.

Sanguinary patches had sunk deep into the grain. I pressed harder, working the bristles in slow circles until my arms burned. The only sounds in the room were the bristles dragging across the floor and the splash of water in the bucket as it slowly turned the colour of expired salmon.

Tucked in his room like a secret, Gunnar made no sound, yet I could feel him, sense his uncertainty. I did not hear the hiss of his words, but rather experienced them. They bore through me, steady as wind, splintering my nerves and tugging my spirit.

He was speaking with someone.

Not Ophelia, no. I could not imagine he'd ever be so emotionally raw with her. This companion, this stranger, felt like someone . . . older. Wiser. Absent.

I stopped scrubbing. The ceiling held me with something close to hypnosis. A woman formed in my mind's eye.

I saw her only in fragments, the way a dream shows a person's features before you wake. A narrow, sharp face. Pale hair braided tight. Eyes pitch as a starless night. She was tall and broad-shouldered. Not beautiful in any gentle sense, but impossible to ignore. The longer you studied her, the more expressive she became.

The moment her eyes fell on Gunnar, she knew he would belong to her. Not from love, not even from desire, but from a deeper and more complicated hunger.

Hunger.

Then she stepped toward him and–

Outside, a car engine rumbled. Tires ground over gravel. The woman in my mind vanished. The vision broke like a popped soap bubble.

My pulse quickened, and for a single, fleeting moment, hope flared. Someone had come—someone passing by the house, maybe from the bank, or perhaps from Sylvie's work.

I wanted to scream, to let them know I was being held here, but my throat strained, and nothing came.

Then the locks on the front door released with a heavy crack.

Ophelia laughed—high-pitched, almost drunken. I knew she was faking it. A man's voice answered. I couldn't catch the words, but Ophelia's were laced with venom. Gunnar shifted upstairs. Something moved with him, subtle, deliberate, as if he had set something back on a shelf.

Ophelia had invited someone to Whitmore.

The stairs creaked as they climbed. Their voices entwined. A request for gin, a prayer for sex without boundaries.

"You don't have to worry," Ophelia assured him. "I'll have you begging for mercy."

He laughed, and the amusement carried as her guest inquired about the lack of light, the sour smell, and where he could relieve himself.

"Right this way."

They stopped outside the master bedroom where I was cleaning.

With the heavy click of the latch, the door opened. I recoiled into the corner, desperate to dissolve into the floral patterns of the Victorian wallpaper, where the shapes gathered into skulls.

He stepped in first. For a moment, the darkness swallowed him, leaving only a silhouette framed by the flicker of candlelight. He stood slightly taller than Ophelia, but wide, heavy through the frame.

From my corner, I could smell him. The tart tang of alcohol clung to his clothes. His breath was mephitic. Sweat soaked into his skin—thick, human, unclean. It gathered in the folds of him, between his legs, along his skin.

But beneath it all, there was hot, hot blood.

Blood . . .

It burned under his flesh. I could feel it from where I sat, heat rolling off him in slow waves. I shouldn't have been able to perceive the brine of him from across the room, but it was a strange new sense of smell, almost an intuitive guess.

The floor lamp clicked on, and everything was cast in a cranberry hue. He winced at the sudden glare, then paled as he took inventory.

Dumbstruck, his gaze tracked the damp patches that faintly smelled of cheap pine cleaner.

The red flecks spattering the wallpaper.

The bed, stripped of sheets.

The mattress, sunken and fetid.

And finally, *finally,* he saw me, and I felt a sense of realism I hadn't experienced since that first frenzied feeding.

"What the fuck is this?" His voice was nails on a chalkboard. Ophelia laughed and gave a small, careless twirl before drifting toward him. The man faltered and stumbled back—straight into Gunnar, who had appeared like a silent assassin.

In a single, fluid motion, Gunnar seized the man by the throat and lifted him off the ground. The man convulsed in his grip, legs kicking into the empty air. Saliva spilt down his chin.

Gunnar raised him higher, tightening his hold until the man's back bowed and he shuddered in breathless bursts.

And then, release.

He hit the floor. His ghastly gurgles mixed with soap.

He barely managed to scramble on all fours. Ophelia stood over him, the knife I'd coveted held loosely in one hand. She forced him to stay down, pressing him forward before swinging herself onto his back, straddling him with practiced ease.

Her weight, still impossible to determine, drove him to the floor. One hand yanked his head back as her legs locked around his torso, urging him forward in jerking, violent motions.

His eyes locked onto mine, huge and glassy, frantic. He strained to shape a plea.

The knife winked.

I smelled it before I saw it—the blood. From across the room, I felt its warmth, its sudden, heavy essence. The heat of it dulled my thoughts, softened them. I couldn't look away. I watched as a thin, pale line appeared on his throat, then widened, before spilling all at once.

I pinched my nose, viced my teeth, but it made no difference. The taste was already there—copper and oil, coating my tongue with something thick and expectant.

He jerked violently, choking, coughing. A grotesque spray of spittle and blood undid all my hard work. His eyes bulged as if they might burst from their sockets.

Ophelia laughed, bright, moving with him as though breaking a wild horse, one arm arcing through the air while the other held him tight.

I wanted to look away, but my eyes refused. Slowly, I slid down the wall until I sank into a seated position. Nausea and fear coiled through me, my chest tight with the sickening spectacle. And yet, I salivated.

Gunnar stood at the door and watched, detached, while Ophelia glowed with the fevered energy of a child on a carousel.

In a final, desperate surge, the man lurched toward me. Ophelia slipped from his back, laughing, the sound too merry for what was happening.

His hand found my ankle. It dragged across my skin, leaving a smear of heat. Then he gave up.

He collapsed at my feet, fingers curling in a phantom reach before pulling back. Ophelia caught his leg and hauled him around, forcing him onto the grain of the wooden planks. With a scream of victory, she threw herself onto him, drinking in deep, greedy gulps.

But it was not enough. The wound was too shallow. She caught the hilt of the knife and drove it home, stabbing harder, deeper, widening the gash until the red overflow was finally thick enough to satisfy her.

Gunnar finally pushed himself from the threshold. He cast a brief, detached glance in my direction before bending over the convulsing body.

In the gloom, their bodies blurred into a desperately ravenous thing.

VIII

Gunnar and Ophelia lay on the sordid sheets beside me, their limbs a tangled geometry of spent skin and salt. Gunnar sprawled on one side, frantically inhaling. Ophelia lay on the other, her leg draped over my hips.

She was streaked with the cooling red of the kill, yet she seemed intoxicated—exhilarated by the blood. She giggled and rolled onto her side.

I was exhausted. They had passed me between them until my joints felt unmoored. My hair hung in clumps where their hands had seized it, and Ophelia moved against me, drawing her pleasure until it shuddered through her.

Then she lingered, her fingers slipping inside me, curling and pressing while my hands scraped against the bedframe. She enticed, stroked, and teased, driving me relentlessly toward the edge until my body betrayed me for the hundredth time. My raspy moans broke into a loud cry that shook the room. Shame flooded me. I had never screamed like that before—never had an orgasm hit so deep, or so raw, that it stripped me of whatever was left of my humanity.

They didn't drink from me. Tonight, they had someone else.

It had only been two nights since I buried the sweaty man Ophelia brought home.

They went out together after sunset. Ophelia wore one of Sylvie's thin floral sundresses—entirely wrong for the tightening cold. To compensate, she threw Sylvie's trench coat over her shoulders. The clothes fit her perfectly.

Now that I was no longer their food, I wondered what would become of me. In this house, to be useless was to be forgotten, and to be forgotten was to be buried.

Gunnar turned his head slightly when Ophelia said, "I want to see Agatha have a drink. Agatha, go on. Try."

I stared at her. She wanted me to do *what*?

"Now, Agatha." She nudged me with a sharp flick.

I rose slowly, trembling.

I approached the corpse, frozen in the shape of its last moments. I knew I had to touch it, but I couldn't.

The wound was a raw, messy cavity. Their teeth had shredded his neck to mince. His head tilted at a grotesque angle, barely held in place. It reminded me of how they'd left Sylvie. Broken and discarded. The metallic stench caught me in its fist. "Try it, Agatha," Ophelia said. "Before it goes cold."

I lowered my face to the wound.

Now.

Do it.

Just fucking do it, and they'll leave you alone.

My lips brushed the torn flesh, slick with blood. I tried to draw from it, tentative at first. Sinew shifted, tough and uneven, the taste of iron so wrong, yet strangely addictive. Something loose caught between my teeth, a shred of skin. It was gelatinous and warm.

I realized too late.

The piece was worming its way down my oesophagus.

I gagged.

The small amount of blood I had taken came up with bile, and when there was nothing left, I kept retching, unable to stop.

Ophelia laughed and clapped her hands, delighted.

Gunnar watched from the bed, his expression unreadable. Then he got up and left, his naked body a formidable, silent shadow moving through the room. He didn't reach for his clothes, leaving the door hanging open as he disappeared into the hall.

I was in hell.

Under Ophelia's eye, I dug the grave—the third one, counting Sylvie. The pit came out shallow. The ground was stubborn, and they no longer seemed to care if the rot was found.

This time, I felt nothing but numbness. The man whose blood I had tasted meant nothing to me. He was merely a waste to be disposed of. Leftovers for the earth and its inhabitants.

Ophelia hovered at the edge of the pit.

"Where's your family?" she asked.

I was mildly surprised when she spoke. I kept digging, concentrating on the soil. She waited a moment, then pressed on.

"You don't speak to them? Are they still alive?"

She allowed the question to hang in the air before moving past it with a shrug.

"Mine are long gone," she said. "And you know what? I don't feel a thing. They were the ones who sold me to *that man . . .*"

Her face twisted, a sudden flash of old hate breaking through.

"Robert," she spat his name out like it was a mouthful of putrescence. "He was awful. And he deserved everything— everything!—he got."

With a soft motion, she reached up to fix a stray curl of hair, surreptitiously wiping a tear from the corner of her eye.

"It was a transaction for my parents. You see, they were rich people. They wanted a son to inherit it all, to continue the business. But they got me. A daughter. To them, I was just a stepping stone to the heir they longed for. So they married me off for profit—*to combine the dynasties*, as per my father's toast at our wedding. My husband raped me the very first night. And though I didn't resist him, he beat me senseless. I was only eighteen."

I wondered why she was sharing her past with me. Why did she suddenly feel the urge to show that side of her, the part of her life where she was a victim? To connect with me better? To garner sympathy?

But it was difficult to feel sympathy for her. She'd used her trauma to carry on her own dynasty of blood and murder.

"I tried to be good for him," she continued. "I truly thought I was doing something wrong, because he just kept at it. Then, after a year, I finally struck back. I hit him with a cast-iron skillet. He died on the spot. And they committed me to an asylum." Her voice shifted, losing its hysterical edge. "And then *he* got me out." Her chin lifted in the direction of Gunnar's room. I couldn't tell if she was grateful for the mercy he'd provided or resentful for the life she now led.

But I was too tired to indulge in the search for answers. I could barely stand. "You need to hurry," she said at last, glancing toward the horizon where the sky had begun to pale into a sickly, translucent gray.

I rolled the body into the grave; it hit the bottom with a muffled thud. Clumps of soil followed him, indifferent.

It had to have been over a month since they locked me in. Trees that had been bright with autumn were bare now, exposing mottled limbs. Nearby, Ophelia admired the hydrangeas that had long since gone brown and rotted on the stalk.

· · ·

I jolted awake, certain someone had screamed directly into my ear.

Wake up!

The demand still echoed in the stagnant air. I could swear a man was in the room—a presence that wasn't Gunnar—but I couldn't decipher any unusual shapes in the sinister shade.

The blood I'd consumed had to be poisoning me.

I rolled onto my side and only then realized I wasn't chained.

In her haste to finish before dawn, Ophelia had forgotten. This was my chance.

A sliver of light slipped through the cracks in the boarded window.

Daylight.

Heaving, I realised they'd kept me drained and spent, until I succumbed to exhaustion, not waking until night. I was never meant to be awake post-dawn.

Looking at the ray of daylight brought a sharp, splintering headache that only fueled the nausea.

I lurched over the edge of the bed and vomited. Bile, streaked with a secondary thread of blood, dribbled to my feet. I stared at the mess, fully expecting the rest of my insides to follow, but the upheaval began to recede. My stomach gave a couple more agonizing twists before settling into a bruised calm.

I forced myself upright, but my body failed me. A sharper wave of sickness hit, and I collapsed, striking the floor hard.

God help me, I prayed, though I did not believe in God any longer.

I lay still, listening, hoping I had not roused my captors.

Somehow, I found a fraction of strength left in my limbs. My arms trembled as I braced myself against the wall and moved slowly down the hall, careful to avoid any creaking underfoot. I didn't know where they were.

Each step was an effort, my whole body shaking, but I kept moving. The hallways seemed longer than I remembered, narrowing into an eternal corridor of torture.

When I reached the staircase, reality warped. The first step was a plunging descent, the pitch too steep. My legs shook as I lowered myself onto the first one, my fingers digging into the scarred wood of the railing. Breaking my neck would have been a mercy.

But the environment was easier here; intrusive streaks of light no longer irritated my eyes.

Every few steps, I stopped and listened, straining for any sound that shouldn't be there.

Centuries seemed to pass as I descended, bracing myself against a fall.

My heart hammered as I neared the bottom. The front door was close—the only one unboarded, the only way out. I could almost taste the freedom.

I could almost feel the sun and the wind against my skin. But at that thought, my throat squeezed painfully, and a spasm ripped through my body. Nonetheless, I reached the door, my fingers trembling as they closed around the knob.

The lock clicked open.

For a moment, I couldn't believe it. If I could make it outside, nothing else would matter. I would run until my legs failed and my lungs burned, until I collapsed into the grass. I would run until my body gave out.

And if I died, at least I would die free.

I pushed the door open, and a dull, gray light swept into the hallway. It was smoother than I had imagined, yet it struck me like a physical force, searing my retinas and wrestling my skull until I was driven back into the shadows of Whitmore House.

I raised my hand to shield my face, but the light poked between my fingers, almost taunting. What vigor I'd felt melted away as I was consumed by relentless exposure. I tried to step forward, but I trembled violently.

My vision wouldn't adjust. Quite the opposite—the longer I looked, the brighter the light became, expanding into a vast, unforgiving white.

The open space beyond stretched too far, too wide. Hollow. I feared I might step into it and be taken, drawn out into something without edges. Every inch forward demanded more than I had left to give.

Panic coiled low in my gut, spilling out roots from my spine. Every instinct urged retreat. And then, I was lingering on the precipice of in and out. Dark and light. Captive and free. The day barely brushed my toes before my body rebelled through some unknown force. Every muscle screamed with a pain I hadn't known could exist. Every nerve ignited as if the light itself burned me from the inside out.

I gathered myself, tried again, dragging one foot forward, then the other. The world outside tilted and spun, and then, the doorframe rushed to meet me.

I wanted to collapse, to crawl back into the narrow corridor and bury myself in the shadows of this filthy house. I wanted to claw the door shut. I wanted to sink back into the small, stagnant safety I knew.

With a shuddering sob, I let the door click shut. The terrifying vacuum of the outside was gone. I dropped to the bottom step, knees drawn up and arms wrapped tight, crying until my chest burned.

I had been outside at night—digging graves, burying the dead.

Why was the daylight so unbearable?

I was a rabid animal at the water's edge—dying of thirst, yet unable to drink. My freedom sat just beyond the door, but my body had been rewired to choke at the sight of it.

This was how Ophelia found me.

IX

I buried six more bodies after that.

They continued bringing new people into the house, unmaking them in a leisurely, vile ritual.

On the blackest nights, I laid them in their forever beds and expanded our small cemetery. I spread the soil over them like a rough blanket, knowing it would never keep them warm. Their rot would make the earth fertile. Oh, the delicate crocuses that might bloom over their chests, should I live to see the spring.

Afterward, Ophelia bathed me and brushed my hair. Then I slept like those I had buried—dreamless and mercifully blank. Not even Sylvie came to me.

I watched them die. I heard them scream. I saw them cut open and consumed while still alive. And yet, somehow, my mind built a cocoon around itself, sealing away what might have broken me. I felt nothing.

Only hunger and obedience.

I stopped eating entirely and took only water. Strangely, it made me feel a little better. The expired food had likely done more harm than good. My innards pulsed with hunger, yet the shaking eased, and the vomiting ceased.

I remained weak, fragile in every joint and tendon. I had lost so much weight that I felt like a hollowed-out shell—just bones and nothing more. Yet the cuts on my body finally closed. They healed into thin, silver strips that faded with each passing night.

Later, when the headache subsided, I thought I remembered the scent of soil, stronger than usual. Cloying. Damp. Old. I remembered her hair tangled with mud. Or perhaps I imagined it. In this house, the mind invented its own ghosts to fill the silence. The whispers and visions that haunted me only grew louder as I weakened. I tried to catch their echoes while digging the graves, but the voices remained entombed within the house. I heard them best in the third-floor bedroom; they faltered on the second, and withered completely when I was elsewhere.

Ophelia never questioned my attempt to flee and never mentioned it again, as if it had never happened. Maybe she was protecting me from Gunnar's fury.

She no longer chained me.

And every night, she called for me.

"Agatha."

I knew it wasn't my name, but by then I could no longer remember what my real name had been.

It was still there, somewhere in the expanse. I felt that if I concentrated hard enough, I could catch the opening syllable and make it mine again. I tried shaping my mouth into different positions, searching for the one that felt right, but the word kept slipping away. It hid behind new memories of the dark, the blood, and the death.

I would end up trying my new name. Tasting it.

Agatha.

It felt like a little black stone, smooth and cold, rolling against my teeth.

Agatha. Agatha. Agatha.

I could no longer tell when the name was in my head or when it was coming from the outside. Sometimes I heard someone's voice through my shallow sleep, but when I opened my eyes, the room was empty.

Perhaps there had never been any whispers to begin with. Perhaps it was only the static of a dying brain, the sound of a mind unravelling.

Agatha.

The voice tore me back to my senses, stronger and louder than ever. I listened, as I always did, but it didn't return.

I could still see remnants of sunlight, and Ophelia must have been resting. There was nothing to do but wait for her arrival.

However, I forced myself out of bed and moved unhurriedly through the house, searching for something that still carried traces of my lost life. Whitmore had changed. Black mold bloomed like blackened veins along the peeling wallpaper, fed by the rain that leaked through the dilapidated roof. In the corners, the boards had gone supple and spongy. With every tentative step I took, they exhaled, turning the air swamp-thick.

Furniture stood displaced at bizarre angles. I could only imagine it had been shifted in the night by a ghostly order. I clicked a few switches, but the electricity was gone. A tree must have fallen on the lines somewhere out on the property; it had happened once before. Sylvie used to see to such things.

Sylvie.

I would go days without thinking of her. But now that a stray thought had slipped into my comatose mind, her image came alive. I grabbed onto it, holding it tight, but it was still receding. The life I once had was a broken mirror, sharp shards all around. Every once in a while, I'd step on one, and it would shimmer with a distant memory that wasn't attached to anything. All those little fragments led me to Sylvie. A vision of her flickered, then dimmed and slipped back into nothing.

But she still lingered in the ache where my heart should have been, as a dull pressure that never eased. I wanted to speak to her now, even to argue, to hear her voice resist mine. It did not matter what we said. To know she was alive, breathing somewhere beyond this house, would have been enough.

I wished I could recall her face. I wished I could hear her call me by my name—by my real name.

But that would never happen again.

Somewhere deeper in the house, water dripped in slow, uneven intervals. I found candles and matches in a kitchen drawer, my fingers too clumsy to obey me. When the flame caught, it shook, perhaps frightened by the sight it revealed. Varying measures of stubborn blood stains led toward the bathroom where I had slit Ophelia's throat. I followed, not looking for anything in particular, just letting the house steer me through its history.

I moved like an old woman, one hand grazing the wall for balance. The plaster felt cold, slightly soft in places. Whitmore itself had begun to putrefy beneath its skin.

Through the open door, a foul smell of feculence, iron, and stagnant water clung to the back of my throat. No one had been here since that night. The shower curtain lay crumpled on the floor, stiff with trapped blood. I sat on the edge of the bathtub and turned the tap. The water only trickled. I twisted it the other way, but the dripping never became a steady flow. The upstairs plumbing still worked, so Ophelia and I might have been able to take our baths for a while longer.

Slowly, I made my way back to the third floor. I wanted to return to my bedroom and wait for her to awaken, but something pulled me toward the last door in the hall, the one next to mine. The voices grew louder. They sounded like a radio dial being spun—broken static cutting between stations, throwing out different languages before snapping away. They came from that room.

Gunnar spent so many hours here, whispering to an unknown entity. The closer I came, the heavier the pressure grew. But this was not the kind of opposition I'd felt with the sun. This was a primal instinct. Fear of punishment for being caught somewhere off-limits. Still, I needed to see what lay within. What secrets did Gunnar harbor here? I rested my forehead against the wood, straining to hear any sign of life within. But the voices ceased the moment I approached.

Nothing.

I pushed the door.

The room was small, with a sloped ceiling that made it feel like the house was hunching in on itself. I assumed it was a library in its heyday. Shelves stretched along the far wall, sporting dust indentations where books had once stood. Instead, human skulls sat in precise rows. They were evenly spaced, staring at me with hollow eyes and toothless grins.

They differed in size and shade. Some were bone-white, while others were discolored with age. Some were missing incisors; others were cracked and jagged. A variation of other bones lay scattered across the shelves.

I counted everything twice. Twenty-three skulls. Five other bones.

They stared, and I had the strangest sensation that they were determining my personality. An odd compulsion pulled me forward. I set the candle in the center of the room. As I moved, it threw shadows that made the skulls grimace.

I reached for one—the one with the most teeth. Its surface was cold and uneven, gritty beneath my fingers, yet not unpleasant. It felt satisfying to trace the orbits, the parietal bones, and the jagged stitches between them. I wanted to shed my skin and stroke the planes of my own skull. Perhaps such intimacy would provide me with an identity.

"Hey there," I whispered. My own voice sounded foreign in the hush.

It responded with a sad grin. At first, I thought touching the bone would be frightening, but it wasn't. There was something almost soothing in the contact, like a memory surfacing from childhood, one where the sun always shone, and your grandparents were alive. In that memory, the light didn't make my throat spasm or my insides shudder. It felt like the end of a school year, when a whole summer stretched ahead, far from everything that made you unhappy.

I lost myself in the sensation, tracing the outline of the nasal ridge and thin sutures. Each touch put me on high alert, as though the skull could somehow recoil.

I intuited his name was Étienne, the beautiful son of silk weavers in a sunlit French town. Étienne had loved spending time with another boy from his village, one with soft golden curls.

Matthieu, the name pinballed through my thoughts.

Étienne had traced those curls when they lay together in the grass fields beyond the village, alone and safe, unafraid of being discovered. He had cried his heart out when Matthieu died of tuberculosis, convinced he would never love again.

But then, he did. The vision of Gunnar moving toward Étienne displaced Matthieu as a mirage, delicate colors dissolving into nothing, and then, the real Gunnar stepped in. He pried the skull from my hands.

I stared at him, tense, every muscle braced for violence—for the clean slice of a neck, for fingers ripping out my heart. I knew he was capable.

But he didn't lunge. Instead, he knelt, setting his candle beside mine.

There was more than caution in his movements. There was gentleness. Love, even. He held the skull, and I saw his eyes—those dead, endless eyes—ease for the first time. Then, reverently, he returned it to the shelf and turned to me.

He caught my elbow in a grip of iron and jolted me upright. I held his gaze until the world beyond his pupils dissolved into infinite space. Unlike Ophelia, whose earthy scent was faint and haunting, Gunnar held the rich aroma of warzone dirt. It was as if the soil itself clung to him in a desperate need to be noticed.

I had intruded into his space, and I knew, with some deep, unspoken understanding, that this mattered to him. This room was his sanctuary, the shelves sacred, the skulls relics.

Finally, he broke eye contact, letting his gaze drift across the skeletal remains, lingering, then returning to me.

"I've lived a long life, Agatha," he said, and it was only now that I detected the faintest trace of an accent.

"I've had many companions. Flesh fades, but *they* persist—bones, souls, all of them still mine."

The skulls seemed to lean toward him in silent oath, burning with something between devotion and accusation.

He kept the bones of his lovers. He didn't let them go, not even in death. I had the strangest suspicion that we walked a similar path in this sense. There had been someone I refused to let go of when they were begging to be freed.

We were both collectors of the departed. We were the stagnant weight that kept our loved ones from the sky, pinning them to the detritus of our own needs.

From somewhere in the deepest recesses of the house, a shrill voice summoned me.

"Agatha!"

Gunnar let go of my arm but remained as still as the rows of skulls, watching as I turned to leave the room.

Ophelia waited. She needed me.

"There you are, Agatha!" Ophelia materialised at the top of the stairs. "Help me with the bath."

We slipped into the tub together, the water broken by shards of candlelight.

She moved closer, her fingers brushing my ribs. She pressed

her nose to my neck and then buried her face in my hair, sniffing like an animal. I froze—then melted into the sensation.

When she pulled away, a deep ache remained where her touch had been. I almost moved to follow her by some reflexive instinct.

"Were you with Gunnar?" she asked, suddenly serious.

I looked at her, and I knew that she knew. I did not lie, but nor did I confirm.

The corners of her mouth twitched as she measured me with calculating eyes. Then she looked up at the shadows stretching on the ceiling.

"It's so silly, carrying all those bones around. I wish he'd just leave them behind." There was jealousy in her tone. Was it because I had been allowed to see the skulls and live? Or because Gunnar favoured them over her?

Her fingers returned beneath the water, and I leaned into her without thinking.

Her hands traced along my neck, and my shoulders, and lower, then paused. Her touch pressed and lingered, contemplative, as though she wanted to know whether the bone beneath my skin was still mine or if I would soon become one of Gunnar's keepsakes.

X

The feast was over. Gunnar had returned to his asylum of the deceased, kneeling among the skulls like a priest before his reliquaries. Ophelia remained in bed, the blood tracing down her in tenebrous rivulets.

Today, she was not in a good mood. She had already been tense, and the fact that this one had died so quickly only spurred her irritation. She had tried to take it out on Gunnar, riding him so fiercely that she never found her own release. He had lost patience, flipping her over to claim his own. He hadn't looked at me once, and he had left right after.

Wanting to comfort Ophelia, I crawled between her legs. The space was slick with her own juices and Gunnar's thick, musky seed. I pressed closer, careful, and latched myself onto her, tasting mostly him.

My tongue strained over the small, firm curve of her bump. I tried to gain momentum, my fingers already reaching for her, but before I could settle, she caught my hair in a grip and wrenched me back. I looked at her in surprise.

"I'm not in the mood," she said flatly, pushing herself off the bed before moving to the bathroom.

Now, the room smelled like a desecrated cathedral of flesh and flame. I propped myself up on my elbows and looked down.

There he lay, mutilated and discarded.

I had seen him alive, if only for the briefest of moments. He was rude and handsy with Ophelia. And then, I watched him die. Somehow, he had never been human to me. The moment he crossed the threshold of the room where I had waited for him in a dim corner, I had already unmade him in my mind. Something inside me had decided he didn't matter long before he was gone.

Perhaps it was the only way to survive—sever the person from the corpse before the corpse had even cooled.

The smell of his innards was hot sugar—so unlike the others.

I crouched, knees cracking, and slid the folded sheet beneath him. I moved mechanically and without emotion, as if I were cleaning a table after a meal or putting dishes away.

My only concern was that this one was heavier than its predecessors. The rigid mass resisted my manipulations. Dragging it was a weary burden.

I stopped halfway, gasping, hands slick. I wiped my face without thinking and tasted salty syrup at the edge of my mouth. Blood.

It had smeared across my skin, blossoming on my tongue like the first flower after a long winter—sweet and bright. It did not taste wrong. Instead, it almost reminded me of a milky liqueur, and I had the faintest recollection of gulping those under the shelter of the gazebo.

Saliva pooled. I began to ache. And then . . . I didn't spit. I swallowed.

The substance lingered on my tongue like salt along the rim of a glass, stinging, strange, and exhilarating. It was making my head spin. I almost giggled from how good it felt.

For a moment, I forgot it had come from this corpse.

In my mind, it had come from God. And God was telling me to take another sip.

I didn't resist.

The next evening, I forced myself up early. It was easy, the energy still bubbling through me. I lay there with my eyes closed and recalled the taste of blood. I toyed with the memory, trying to summon it, until a sudden burn and a harsh, chemical tang made me spit. Blood coated my lips, and I realized I had bitten my own tongue. Why did my own blood taste so foul and acidic?

But never mind that now. Drawn by the same strong pull, I reached the room with the skulls and entered without hesitation, fueled by this newfound power.

The house was quiet, the world outside sinking into sleep, and Gunnar and Ophelia had not stirred.

When they awoke, there was always music, the friction of bodies, or Ophelia's endless preaching about Gunnar's indifference, or her ceaseless chatter about her misery with her parents, and then her husband, and the asylum.

I could not believe they had lived so long, and yet so little. It was all death, and sex, and eternal ruin.

But this was my time. This was when the world belonged to me.

Settling in with the warmth of a single candle, a tentative brush of my hand over the skulls and bones sent shivers through me once more. It felt as if they were returning the caress, accepting me as one of their own.

I lingered over Étienne. Something in him called to me. I carefully plucked the skull from the shelf and settled with him on the floor.

He told me how Gunnar had found him, how he had been seduced by the shape of his face, the mysteries in his silences. Gunnar had welcomed him into the night, and they had spent an eternity together, watching the world drift by in its chaotic rush. Étienne had wished it could always remain like that, unchanging. Endless.

But life rarely offered such grace.

Gunnar had grown restless, weary of the same hunting grounds, the same shadows. Staying in one place became too risky, and he decided to cross into the new world. Étienne had refused. He couldn't fathom spending months on a cankered boat, surrounded by salt water and hunger. He loved his homeland and swore he would never leave. Never.

And then he did. Though against his will.

Voices and music curled upstairs, spreading through the house like smoke. There was a snap, a fleeting moment of freefall, and then I broke from my trance. The boy disappeared, his blue eyes replaced by a piece of bone, the empty sockets staring at me with infinite sadness.

Étienne slipped from my thoughts, his story left unfinished. I hesitated with his skull still cupped in my hands. I silently pleaded that he not make a sound, to keep our meeting a secret. In return, I would share nothing of what he'd shared with anyone. He agreed, but no one was coming. I set him back on the shelf among his comrades, and stepped outside.

I wanted to vanish into my room, but Gunnar and Ophelia were right at the base of the stairs. One step, and they would hear me. So I stayed fixed in place.

"You are always there, with those bones." Ophelia was shouting. "It's like they're more precious to you than I am! As though their company is preferable to mine!"

He didn't answer.

I knew Gunnar's silence. It was more terrifying than any words. His stillness was of a predator, poised to pounce.

"I know you only got me to replace your dear Étienne! But he did not want you! I do! Haven't I followed you everywhere?

Haven't I done everything for you? Why am I not enough? He is dead! I'm alive!"

The heat drained from my face. *Étienne*. The name I had given the skull. But I had never spoken it aloud.

I had thought I had invented him, or perhaps hallucinated him, trapped in a prison of my own mind and driven mad by the things I had seen and done. But no. He had been waiting for me to find him, to hear him.

"This is why I wanted to keep her. Because you are not there for me! You cannot take her too! Please don't take her! Let me have her!"

Foolish Ophelia. In all her long, sprawling life, she'd learned nothing. *Nothing!* She did not understand that Gunnar was not a man to be moved by tears or the frantic discord of a plea. She was unmaking the delicate peace we had carved, throwing her tantrums into the half-dark and ensuring that the merciless weight of his attention fell first and heaviest into the very thing she wanted to keep.

Me.

Sobs cut through the music, followed by the sound of approaching steps. Gunnar was nearing.

Panicking, I stepped back into the room with the bones, knowing well enough how idiotic the idea was. This was where he would come. He would find me here once again.

And now, with Ophelia acting as she was, discussions of ending me were bound to continue.

I gripped the handle with both hands, my knuckles white as I fought to keep the lock from clicking. But the moment the door met the frame, it was ripped from my grasp. I stumbled back, my heart hammering as Gunnar's enormous frame loomed over me. In the clotted dark, he was nothing but a silhouette, yet I found myself leaning into the space where his eyes—two black holes—should have been.

The thick scent of disturbed soil turned the room into a tomb, and every breath I drew felt like a mouthful of graveyard dirt.

The front door slammed with a force that rattled the house's foundation. The jagged cough of a motor broke the night. Tires clawed over gravel. Then, the sound of the retreating car dwindled into the distance.

Ophelia was gone.

I discerned weeping.

Shaken, I turned toward the skulls.

It was them. The bones were weeping. *For me?*

I looked back at Gunnar, wondering if he heard it too.

He was approaching with a terrifying, measured grace. I had nowhere left to run. When the space between us vanished, he seized my wrist and twisted my back to him. He drove my face toward the shelves. A short scream escaped me, more from the shock than the pain. My cheek pressed against the bones. I didn't need to see them to know who they were.

One belonged to the woman I had seen before, the Viking. The only one who had chosen Gunnar, not the other way around. The bone was splintered, a serrated shard at one end where it had been snapped like dry kindling.

The other was also a woman, older, her gaze steady, knowing. Her lips were pressed into a thin line, the skin around them pulled taut as a drumhead. She seemed to watch me, slowly shaking her head, whether in judgment or regret, I couldn't tell.

I remembered the tale of Bluebeard and his curious wives, how each had entered the forbidden cellar only to find the bodies of those who came before. It had been a test, and their prize for curiosity was to join the collection.

My head was already positioned perfectly on the shelf; all that remained was for him to snap it from my body.

"They speak to you," Gunnar growled against my ear.

How had it not occurred to me that I wasn't the only one who heard them?

They spoke to both of us. It was why we kept coming here. The bones were calling to us.

But not to Ophelia.

I forced myself to relax, and as the rigidity left me, I felt his grip lessening too, his hand sliding from a shackle to an anchor.

I turned to face him, refusing to die without seeing my opponent. In the same heartbeat, he claimed my lips. It was not a caress, nor the crude force I had spent my life evading. It was a harvest. A dark communion in which he did not merely take, but consumed. He fed on the air in my lungs, drew the marrow from my bones, tasted something that felt like the root of my soul. And yet he allowed me to take from him as well, offering something he had never given before: himself.

For the first time, I was held as something of terrible and singular value, possessed with an intensity that stripped me bare.

His hands found the hem of Ophelia's gifted peignoir, bunching the fabric upward as he hoisted me against the shelves.

He pried my legs apart. The dead shifted faintly behind me, letting me take space among them.

A terrifying new sensation unfurled—a frantic, buried craving I had never known. I wanted it. I wanted *him*. Body and mind. He was the first person I had ever shared a secret with, the first to truly hold me. And I desperately needed more. I wanted him to reach inside me and scoop everything else out, leaving only the sacrament of our union.

When he entered me, the stretch was sharp, tearing through the numbness. I forced my thighs to loosen, to yield—to accept the thick, heavy weight of him just as they had before. He filled me so completely it reached far beyond flesh. He was reshaping me from the inside out, deepening the intimate knowledge between us with each brutal thrust, swelling until there was no room left to breathe.

The bones continued their wild dance, spurred by the relentless driving of a monster they no longer served.

XI

They were fighting again. I only heard Ophelia, but I could feel Gunnar growing frustrated and angry. I didn't just interpret how he felt; somehow, I experienced his curdling rage as if it were my own. Ophelia's behavior and her capricious inclinations were washing away the beauty he had once been so drawn to.

Now his energy was pushing her away. She sensed it and fought vigorously, refusing to accept that their time was coming to an end. Sylvie had once told me the same thing, that maybe our time was over, and we only made sense for a while. She told me she felt as if we were only held together by the house. I'd refused to believe it.

But Gunnar and Ophelia were different. There was no potential to be found there. Like two old spouses, they moved in inertia while one of them drifted away. I was not sure which one. I wondered if Gunnar would just leave one day, leaving Ophelia and me alone in a house that stood on bones, with the ghosts of people we had killed.

The skulls were aloof today, all except Étienne. He was a gentle boy, and neither time nor death could wash that away.

We had grown so close and shared so much. Even though he resented Gunnar with all that remained of him, he still loved him.

Étienne whispered to me. He told me how tiresome it had been to always carry the earth with them, how he had had to wear it on his body and return to the soil of his home during the day to restore himself. It all made sense then. The lockets Gunnar and Ophelia wore held soil that bound them to their homes.

I retreated to my own room and shut the door. I curled up on the bed and traced the dark folds of the sheets, trying to still my thoughts while the mood of the house pressed in.

Not long after, Ophelia slipped in, damp and disheveled from the storm outside. Her eyes were rimmed with tears that glinted in the dim candlelight. She didn't say anything at first. She just stood there with her chest heaving. Then she spoke, her voice low with a dangerous lilt.

"I've had enough," she murmured, and I could only guess what lay behind those words.

She stepped closer. I sensed the hunger in her, but it was not just for blood. It was for control and for release, for something that had slipped through her fingers over centuries. I took the brush and sat her down by the mirror, then gently untangled her hair. It had not grown an inch in the months since she'd arrived.

I traced the shape of her head with the soft bristles and thought about how Gunnar would do it, if he would even do it at all. Because he had had enough, too. She finally relaxed, and the tears ceased. She caught my hand and cradled her cheek in my open palm.

"Agatha," she whispered like a prayer, and then she said nothing else.

In that quiet understanding, I felt a dangerous kind of satisfaction.

The balance was shifting.

Ophelia didn't come back until almost dawn, but Gunnar showed no signs of worry.

We had never been close without Ophelia's arrangement or direction until recently, and it was strangely arousing. We were back in the bone sanctuary, and I had suspected he liked them watching. Not that they could judge. They were dead. Yet there was something intimate, more intimate than the sex itself, in lying among his former lovers, forcing them into a kind of silent voyeurism. We lay on the floor, my hand trailing across his skin where the dark hair felt coarse under my palm. It was so human that it felt staged, as if he fashioned himself to pass for a man.

I had always had thick black hair on my body, too. At school, girls had laughed at me during gym class. Growing up poor, I had never dared ask my parents to spend money on something like a razor. They would have said no. But I had also been ashamed, too embarrassed even to ask.

So I'd stolen a razor from the local shop and used it for two years, even after it had gone dull and begun tearing at my skin.

Periods, hair, cramps, childbirth, bowel movements—I had hated everything that made us human. It had all seemed so crude, so humiliating.

Sylvie had been the first to teach me to accept myself, to stop flinching from my own body. She had told me pubic hair was normal, that I didn't have to remove it. So I stopped. Periods were simply a part of life. There was nothing wrong with them. They did not make me dirty.

Everything, absolutely everything that had to do with bodies had been beautiful in her eyes. She had loved people. And for a while, I had loved them too.

It was a notion I found myself reconsidering as I studied Gunnar.

He was naked; the only thing on him was his pendant. He noticed me looking, and didn't withdraw when I traced it with my fingers. "The earth from my motherland," he said.

He wrapped my hand in his and squeezed, pressing the pendant into my palm until it hurt.

"Do you feel it? Do you feel the cold?"

The metal didn't warm beneath our hands. On the contrary, it seeped like frost into my skin, as though Gunnar kept a piece of winter there.

"The land was stone and hunger. The air smelled of salt and blood. We built our houses from whale ribs and prayed to gods who did not listen. The nights lasted months. The sun returned, but we never trusted it."

He closed his eyes, and I did the same as he continued.

"The fjords. The black water beneath the cliffs. The way we pushed our dead into the sea and watched the current carry them away." His fist tightened around mine, but I made no sound. "The soil remembers too. And the soil you call home remembers you. You cannot leave it unless you carry some with you. Wherever you go, it must stay with you."

His confessions must have roused him, for he was on top of me then, his girth edging me to the brink. Gunnar watched me closely as I came undone, and afterward he studied me, waiting for me to betray even the slightest flicker of thought. The balance between the three of us was shifting, something subtle beginning to fracture. What would I do about it?

Nothing. I would do nothing at all.

When it was over, and the skulls had borne silent witness to our union, I slipped out for a bath, leaving him alone. We were keeping secrets from Ophelia now, and I didn't know what to do with that knowledge.

At the sharp clap of the front door, I stirred and pulled

myself out of the tub, hoping Ophelia wouldn't smell him on me.

The water had gone cool faster than expected. Late autumn was seeping through the walls, and the house held the cold like a mausoleum. A new leak had opened in the roof, but nobody cared about the drip of water. What was another rotting wall when the entire world had already spoiled?

Dripping, I plucked one of Ophelia's nightgowns from the vanity where she'd shed it like skin. She wore them and abandoned them wherever she pleased. This one bore faint bloodstains, but I didn't mind. If anything, it softened my scent. The silk clung to my damp limbs, raising a scatter of goosebumps. I hurried to compose myself, but also to go to her. I knew she needed me.

At the top of the stairs, I froze again, not daring to descend.

A man. I could smell him from here. His deodorant, his aftershave, the warmth of his skin. Musky, substantial, like a bowl of thick beef stew left to simmer.

The scent stirred something within me, like a snake lifting its head at the promise of prey. I knew this man's fate, that before dawn I would be dragging his corpse through desanctified halls, racing the first light. And yet, his presence filled me with a quiet thrill. His voice, his laughter, warmed the house for a fleeting hour, giving it the fragile illusion of life. I felt a feverish pulse of excitement, knowing he would be unmade soon.

Drawn by the scent, I went downstairs, flying over the steps with ease. I stopped in the murkiness of the second-floor hall, a vantage point where I could watch them clearly without being seen.

He was tall, nearly Gunnar's height, with a robust chest and rugged hands. At first glance, I could have mistaken him for the bone whisperer himself. Ophelia had brought this one as a petty act of defiance. A provocation. She intended to have him killed right in front of her companion.

I almost groaned in disdain. Her games were shallow.

"You live here alone?" the man asked, marveling at the house. Only a few candles lit the hall where he stood.

"My sister lives here too," Ophelia said. She tipped her chin toward the gloom of the upper landing, where I remained a hidden presence.

He flicked the light switch on the wall, but nothing happened.

"The power's out," Ophelia explained.

"What's that smell?"

She didn't answer. Instead, she guided him upstairs. His footsteps dragged. I sensed the shift, the unease unfurling in him. Ophelia quivered in anticipation as the darkness gathered around them. Part of me wondered whether it was a presence she and Gunnar carried, or a being of its own. The comforting warmth of candlelight seemed to snuff out beneath its probing tongue.

"Hey, ah—" he faltered, his brow knitting as he fought to dredge her name from the fog of alcohol. "Olivia. Right. I think I should go."

Ophelia snapped a sharp, "No!" Then, she forced a smile and poured honey into her voice. "Stay. It's going to be so much fun."

He faltered, trying to pass her, but she blocked him, pressing him back until his spine collided with the railings.

"Agatha!" she called.

She knew I was there, lingering on the precipice.

I stepped into the trembling circle of light.

The man jerked back, eyes wide. "What's going on? Let me go, you crazy bitch!"

Ophelia pinched the wick, killing the flame with two fingers, and her devilish smile extinguished with it. The man broke. He bolted up the stairs in a frenzied panic.

The tremor in him—I could almost taste it, feel it!

The way his power slipped through his fingers made my head spin. He still didn't know he wasn't leaving this house alive. But I did.

And I could hardly wait.

He brushed past me. I didn't stop him; I only turned and slowly followed him into the ever-darkening hall.

The game had begun. He could run if he wanted. We would chase him down collapsing stairs and into hollow rooms. But he would never escape.

I should have felt terror. I should have felt guilt. But the human responses in me were long dead. My only way to survive was to join the horror.

I laughed quietly to myself, jittery with excitement. His panic lit Whitmore like fire. He pounded down the hall, hands outstretched, fumbling for doors that would not open, walls that would not give way. It all filled me with unnatural joy.

Maybe it was Ophelia's doing, pushing it into my veins like poison. Or maybe it was just me. Maybe I had always been this way.

He rounded the corner and vanished from view. The secondary staircase lay in that direction, and Ophelia and I followed, our pace quickening even though there was nothing to fear. Every door leading outside was sealed shut, save for the main entrance, and there was no way he would make it back there. He was a cornered animal, stumbling into the anatomy of a house that was preparing to eat him.

We froze when we rounded the corner.

Gunnar was holding our meal by the throat, his fingers digging into the bulge of his neck.

It didn't matter that the pair were equally built. Gunnar hoisted him from the floor with no visible effort. The man's boots kicked uselessly, but no one paid him any mind.

"I told you not today," he said to Ophelia.

She howled. "He is mine!"

Gunnar did not flinch. His eyes were embers. "*Nothing* here is yours."

The neck snapped like a twig.

The writhing stopped.

For a moment, the man stiffened, muscles trembling as if every fiber fought to stay alive. Then his body went slack. Gunnar dropped him to the floor and stepped over the remains. He passed Ophelia and me, and melted into the gloom, leaving nothing but a trail of cold contempt.

Ophelia stood perfectly still, her frame trembling slightly. She pressed the cold knife to her chest as though she were hugging it for warmth.

The game was over.

We didn't touch the body. Gunnar's tone had been absolute, and not even Ophelia, wild and untamed as she was, dared to disobey. Her punishment was hunger.

Mine too.

As I laid turf over the body, hunger clawed at me.

I hated this man. I hated how his death was useless and purposeless. He hadn't lost any blood; he had died for nothing.

Ophelia paced along the edge of the grave but wouldn't speak to me. She was erratic, already making plans in her mind. It was in the way she would stop and freeze, then continue pacing—back and forth, back and forth, like a pendulum.

Finally, she lost her patience. Or perhaps she wanted to speak with Gunnar alone.

Apologize?

No, that didn't sound like her.

She tossed over her shoulder, "Finish here and then come help me in the bath."

I was left alone in the wide expanse of the garden. I could have run. I could have gone as far as possible, called for help, or called the police. But I didn't. Frozen in place, I watched her disappear into the house, and the second the door closed behind her, I threw the shovel to the ground, fell to all fours, and started clawing with my hands—digging and digging until they found the body.

An arm. I pulled back the sleeve of his shirt and brushed the dirt from his skin. Without a second thought, I sank my nails into the flesh.

There was a reason Ophelia and Gunnar used knives. The skin was thick and rigid. My teeth couldn't break it. I tugged and gnawed, desperate, but it barely gave.

I licked my tears.

I was so hungry.

But there was no way I could bite through the skin and get to the blood in time.

The night had been relentless, and my mind buzzed with the fever of it all. Now, all I wanted was to eat.

Yet the moment I was done, I was back in the room with the bones.

Étienne waited for me. His skull sat on the shelf, polished smooth from my fingers. As soon as I touched him, he flooded my mind. He was hungry, too. He starved for communication, and no one else would answer him.

Gunnar wanted only to talk about himself, his endless stories of the old days, each tale a mirror of his own pride and longing. Étienne had grown bored with it, sick of the ceaseless recollections of wealth, conquest, and eternal nights.

He wanted me now. He wanted someone who would listen.

I cradled him like a lover, and spoke softly, though no one else could hear. The room pressed in around me, the shadows of the skulls leaning toward me to listen. Étienne told me stories of the world before the new world, of smells and sunlight and colors that did not exist now. He spoke of love and loss in tones I could almost feel as if they were my own.

Not all the bones spoke to me. Some remained stubbornly

silent. Like the skull with no teeth, blackened with age—it had never whispered a word. But others, I met in fleeting breaths of memory, voices curling like smoke through my mind.

Isolde, Gunnar's lover from the 13th century. A daughter of a knight from a small village in the Holy Roman Empire. She ran away one night, slipping from the strict watch of her mother as the household slept.

She met him at a fair, a stranger cloaked in night and charm, and let him lure her into the woods, let him drink her blood. Like me, she didn't die. When he was sated, she raised her hand, cradled his face, and offered a weak smile despite the torture and abuse.

She became so much more than his companion. She hunted for him, luring people—mostly women, as she was too intimidated by men—for him to drink and use as he pleased, even if it hurt her. That was what Gunnar did to all his lovers. He made them serve.

Their love, if it could be called that, lasted only thirty years. She grew tired quickly. The hunting was eating away at her. She hated seeing them suffer and longed to grant them a painless end.

But not with Gunnar.

Whenever he discovered a fear that you could not conquer, he made you endure it until you lost all sensitivity, until every spark of life was drained from you. Torturing of an arachnophobe with spiders. Forcing a claustrophobe in a coffin.Whether he did it for growth or simply because he relished the sight of his lovers' suffering was unknown.

Isolde tried to run. But no one outran Gunnar. Born a Viking, he took pride in the fact that no enemy, no companion, had ever slipped from his grasp.

He killed her, and like all those he claimed, he kept her head. A trophy. Another piece in his harem of death.

There, a single bone, unmistakably from an arm. I picked it

up, pale and cold, and held it against my own, trying to imagine how it had once fitted, how it had moved, how the flesh and muscle must have stretched and bent over it. I traced its curves and ridges, reconstructing a ghost in my mind. It had belonged to Helvig, someone far older than Isolde. Much, much older.

She had met Gunnar at a frozen fjord, a place he would return to centuries later, drawn by sudden homesickness. She was captivated by the power radiating from him. He was nothing like the other men in her village. She went with him willingly.

After decades, Helvig grew restless. Something in the world beyond Gunnar called to her. She fled one night, and what happened next remains unknown to her. Gunnar hunted her relentlessly, following her scent, tracing her trail. Her death had been so absolute, so final, that she had no recollection, no clue as to what had happened. All that remained of her was the stiff knowledge of who had done it.

These bones were loud. They screamed. Not with sound, but with emotion, with the weight of everything they had endured and were forced to relive every day, unable to rest in peace.

XII

The ache piercing my body was as vicious as the flu. I was shivering and sweating. The pressure from the bed sheets was bruising; the mattress assaulted my back. Worst of all was the knocking in my ears, heavy and persistent, as if someone were driving nails into my head with a hammer.

I tried to lift myself from the bed, but it felt like digging my way out of a deep grave. It must have still been day outside.

Knock. Knock. Knock.

The sound was unbearable. It would not stop.

I moaned, willing it away.

But it came again, stronger this time.

Knock. Knock. Knock.

Then, again, but only twice.

Knock. Knock.

I forced my eyes open through the pain. Light seeped through the shuttered window. Even looking at it made me nauseous. It was too early.

It wasn't in my head.

Someone was knocking.

Outside. At the front door.

Someone was here!

I forced myself up, but my legs refused to serve me, twisting the wrong way. I collapsed onto the floor.

Knock! Knock! Knock!

More persistent this time.

I pushed forward and crawled. Only in the hall did I manage to pull myself onto my feet, holding to the wall for support.

Were they looking for me? Or for Sylvie?

A police officer. A mailman. Someone from Sylvie's work. A friend. A neighbor.

Or perhaps someone was searching for one of the deceased.

They could arrest me. What if they thought I was lying? What if they refused to believe I had been a hostage, forced to bury bodies?

It didn't matter.

Someone had come.

My hands scraped along the warped wood.

Move. Move. Move, I ordered myself.

The stairs loomed before me like a cliff, each step a battle. I had walked just fine the day before, but now I had regressed to the state of someone close to dying. Or was it just the daylight outside?

My fingers found the railing, and I forced myself down the stairs, risking a fall with every step. Nausea rolled through me in heavy waves.

The house was silent, but the knocking lingered, giving me strength and pressing me onward.

Please don't leave, I begged silently. *Wait for me. I'm coming.*

At last, I reached the bottom. The door stood ahead, and my vision narrowed around it, everything else dissolving into the edges of my sight.

Something in me rebelled against investigating.

What if I had imagined the caller? I would open the door only to be punished by light for nothing.

Knock. Knock. Knock.

The door rattled beneath my hand.

It was real.

Someone was really here.

I choked back bile and pushed, inching the door open. The moment it gave way, light exploded, blinding and searing. It was raining outside; the sound of it, the smell, made my senses wild. The sky must have been clouded gray, yet to me it felt like a burning lamp shining at a million watts. My lids squeezed shut, tears spilling, stinging as they traced hot lines down my face.

Against my will, I pushed the door shut, but it rebounded and opened again.

I jerked backward on instinct. The gaping white opening pulled at me like a shattered plane window mid-flight. I reached blindly for the staircase, my fingers closing around the splintered railing as though it were an anchor. *I can't. I can't do it!*

"Jesus, are you okay?" A voice cut through the white noise in my ears, and at the same moment, a merciful shadow positioned itself between me and the punishing light. "The doorbell's not working—"

"Close the door," I croaked.

The door slammed shut, and I collapsed onto the floor, drenched in cold sweat, every muscle shaking.

How would I ever escape this house if my reaction to the day only grew worse? I hadn't seen daylight in so long. My body reacted violently to even the faintest hint of it. Something was seriously wrong with me.

"Is Sylvie here?" the voice, in which I now recognized a feminine cadence, continued to ask.

"Who the fuck are you?" I struggled to focus on the figure as it drifted in and out of clarity.

The woman stood tall, short black hair framing her face.

"It's Rochelle. I am . . ." she faltered, her gaze shifting to the side, ". . . a friend of Sylvie's?"

Why the fuck was she saying it like a question?

Rochelle. The name stirred something in my faded memory.

I knew her. I knew of her.

Rochelle. Sylvie had once talked about her, and then stopped. *Rochelle,* who sent those late-night texts that the love of my life so solemnly insisted were strictly work-related. *Rochelle,* whose name escaped in a soft giggle whenever Sylvie was on the phone while hiding in the bathroom or lingering outside for a smoke, thinking she was alone. *Rochelle,* who had moved to London, climbing higher and higher up the corporate ladder, just as Sylvie's mood had soured in a strange coincidence.

That Rochelle.

The woman stepped closer. "Iris, right?"

Who is Iris? My inflamed brain struggled to keep up. But the name sounded almost familiar.

Almost like it was . . .

"Is Sylvie here? I just got back from London and learned she stopped coming into work months ago. Is she okay? Did she move?"

She had come for Sylvie. Like she had any right! How had she gotten this address? Had she been here before?

Rochelle sniffed the air. Her nose twitched, noting the foulness.

"What's that smell?" she asked, and then again, "Is she here or not?"

I could think of nothing but my hatred for the woman in front of me. It swallowed everything inside me, everything around me. Even the ever-present hunger faded beneath it.

The hatred fueled me, gave me strength. I straightened my

back. If I couldn't go outside, I could at least show her what lay within.

"Yes," I said in barely a whisper. "Yes, she's here. You drove here?"

"No, I took a cab," she said absentmindedly, too distracted to grasp why I was asking.

I pushed myself upright, still gripping the railing, and took in the woman's appearance. She was not unattractive, but she was not Sylvie's type. Sylvie had always gone for long-limbed, dark-haired, grungy princesses. Like me. Like all her girlfriends before me.

I still had my black hair, now longer than ever, but I was wrapped in the silk slips I had been wearing for months, making me look nothing like myself. Making me Agatha instead of what I used to be. *Who* I used to be.

I was probably no longer Sylvie's type either.

Not that it mattered any more.

"Help me to the back," I murmured. "She's over there, on the terrace."

"Are you sick?" Rochelle's fingertips hovered over my shoulder as if I might infect her.

Above us, two floors up, the bones were vibrating, a chorus of hunger and anticipation so loud I feared she would hear. But Rochelle noticed only the house's distress, her face growing more troubled, yet she never turned back. I led her in, lured her forward. Past the bloodied wood and carpet. Past the ichor curdling in the corners. Past the fungus spreading behind the wallpaper, veins beneath diseased skin.

Rochelle had no idea. She didn't know the back terrace had already given way, the boards collapsing like a broken ribcage.

I led her, turning back now and again to catch her scent. Beneath her floral perfume and the faint trace of hair gel, I could smell her blood, spiced and sugary. I saw the large vein pulse in her neck. The drum of her heartbeat grew louder. I could taste her sweetness in the air.

I licked my lips. Inhaled deep.

The smell. *God, that smell.*

It was too late by the time I came back to my senses.

I could feel my pupils slowly contracting back to their normal size. The salt of Rochelle's blood coated my mouth, and my tongue worked to gather it all into a swallow.

There was a gurgling to my left side. I rolled drunkenly toward Rochelle's unblinking stare. Her body twitched, a reflex, as the vigor oozed out of her.

The chef's knife lay further away in the pool of thick liquid.

So this was how she went.

I had drunk so much I feared my stomach might split. But it felt so. damn. good.

I closed my eyes in a haze of bliss.

Fuck Rochelle.

No one stood between Sylvie and me. No one!

The sun leaned toward the horizon. That was when I slowly began to descend from the high.

Panic hit me in waves, crashing harder with every thought. Not that I had killed someone. No, that barely registered. But what if someone came looking for her? What if her coworkers, her family, the people who loved her, followed her trail here? What would I do with her body?

And most urgent, most terrifying: *what if Gunnar and Ophelia found out?*

They mustn't. This would be the end of me.

I couldn't go outside. The sun was still up.

The cellar. I could put her there. I just needed to break the padlock and hide her from sight. The house already stank of death. What was another note in the symphony of rot?

I stumbled through the kitchen, my mind racing in crooked circles. Fuck, now bloodied footsteps were dotted everywhere.

I didn't know what to do first. Clean? Move her? It felt like trying to solve an equation with too many steps while racing against time. Everything seemed urgent. Everything at once.

Plastic. I needed to wrap her in plastic.

I thought of the bloodied, molded curtain in the bathroom on the first floor, then remembered the plastic sheets in the living room, rolled up and forgotten from when we tried to renovate.

I tore through the space, nearly tripping over a chair, ripping open the roll with shaking hands.

It was still there, folded in a dusty corner like it had been waiting for this moment. I could wrap her in it, keep her contained, keep the smell from rising, at least long enough to think.

Back in the kitchen, her body lay open, slack and leaking. I had drank like a leech, but I could only hold so much. Now, the remaining blood kept weeping from the chaotic network of wounds across her body. Had I done all that? Had I stabbed her again and again in a hungry rage?

If the stains remained, if they found out... I was finished.

I laid the plastic in the corridor and began dragging her body onto it, trying to keep the blood from staining the cover on the outside. Her weight was unbearable, dead flesh heavier than anything living. The plastic shifted, sliding across the already blood-smeared wooden floor. I sobbed desperately as my hands lost their grip again.

Then, at last, she was wrapped in several layers of furniture protection. I lifted her by the feet and dragged her to the basement door. I tried to keep the trail tight, to contain the spill, but crimson streaks followed anyway.

Once there, I pushed the body down the stairs. There was no way I was hauling it down. I needed to preserve some energy.

At the bottom, the darkness was a solid thing. I swore under my breath and went back upstairs to fetch a light.

I ran in circles, searching for something to break the padlock —a baseball bat, an axe, a shovel.

A shovel! There was one hiding in the corner, and I'd only found it when I stumbled and hit the floor.

The hatch sat in the opposite corner of the basement, but a closer look brought me to a halt. There was no lock. The circles of the hinged hasp were broken off, too. I didn't remember doing it. But I didn't remember many things. So many memories had already become blank spaces in my mind.

I lowered myself to the floor, placing the metal edge against the boards with a trembling hand to stifle any clatter. The hatch was a predatory jaw clamped shut, but I gripped the handle and pulled.

The void exhaled a thick draft of soil onto my face. It coated my tongue and settled in my lungs. I stared down at the stairs, watching them disappear into a darkness that felt eternal.

I descended carefully, and the small opening below revealed two wooden boxes, pressed into the space between walls lined with old shelving.

They were shaped like coffins.

A cold thrum of dread crawled down my spine.

I dropped to my knees and tried to lift the lid of one box. It budged, uncovering a familiar face. Buried under a layer of soil, Ophelia slept. Only her face, the top of her chest, and her feet were visible.

Jesus fucking Christ.

Every instinct screamed to run, but I couldn't. I was rooted there, staring at her lair, knowing I had crossed a line I could never uncross.

This was why there was always a hint of soil in the scent they gave off. This was why Ophelia always bathed before coming near me. She hadn't wanted me to know.

She lay before me, her lips a bluish hue. She looked so innocent, so young. So harmless.

My heart squeezed at the sight.

I returned the lid to its place and retreated quietly.

Fuck Rochelle, I thought, dragging her body back to the main floor. Time was slipping away, and I was running out of options. At least I had checked first. It saved me from blindly shoving the corpse into the unknown. At least she hadn't brought her own car, for whatever reason. It would be hard to dispose of, given I couldn't leave the house while my captors were resting. Thank God for small favors.

Once back in the hall, I adjusted the plastic, rewrapping her as tightly as I could. I used an entire roll of tape to secure her makeshift body bag, trying to keep the worst of it contained.

Think, goddamn it, think!

When we moved in, the house had been filled with custom wardrobes. The previous owners had tried to sell them to us, and when we refused, they asked if they could leave them behind. We agreed—and I would never stop regretting it. They were screwed deep into the walls, and removing them would be a much bigger project than we'd anticipated. Now, their empty vessels would be my salvation.

I opened one and pushed the bundle of flesh and plastic inside. For a moment, I thought I had it positioned just right— until it slipped, sliding partway out before I could grab hold. I forced the bulk back in before slamming the door shut. I leaned against it, exhaling.

For now, I was safe.

I prayed on one of the coming nights that I would get a chance to bury the evidence.

Speaking of . . . I had to clean up.

We never brought bodies into the kitchen or living room, so those areas remained unsullied. It was the staircase from the first to the second floor that bore the stains—bodies were dragged down it regularly.

Now, the kitchen looked like a slaughterhouse. I had only a handful of minutes before the sun set, and I needed to hurry—stairs, basement, everything.

I scrubbed and cleaned, my hands red and raw, the blood still showing. Forgetfully, I sucked some of it off a knuckle that had just split, and it burned my throat. *What the fuck?*

I spat it out, gurgling, the pain slowly subsiding. Had there been chemicals on my arms that I accidentally swallowed? But no—I hadn't used any. Just soap. Sylvie had always been opposed to chemicals, and we never kept any at home. Only natural detergents.

Was it my own blood?

When they woke, I was in the room with bones, trying to calm myself. Étienne had been soothing me, whispering that it was okay, that none of this was my fault. They had starved me, turned every sense against me.

I sat just outside the candle's glow, where the trembling light blurred into deep shadow. I cradled him in my lap, my fingers tracing the smooth, cold curve of his brow.

What do I do?

Do nothing, he answered—a rustle of dead leaves in a cold, winter wind. *People always think they need to do something when it's best to do absolutely nothing.*

I turned that over in my mind, stroking the edges of his cranium as if he were a lap dog.

Does it hurt? Being like this?

He went quiet, the skull's features taking on an almost thoughtful air in the flickering light.

Nothing hurts more than being forced into an existence you don't want.

Gunnar paused in the doorway. His eyes swept over me. Could he hear my heartbeat, pounding faster and faster? Could he hear our clandestine whispers? Did he know about my deception? I didn't falter. I met his gaze, challenging his opinion for the first time.

"It smells like soap downstairs," he said, almost bored.

I didn't answer.

XIII

É tienne's first kill had come months after he had joined Gunnar. He resisted the easy prey Gunnar urged him toward—old men, lonely women, the weak who would not fight back. It felt dishonorable, he said, almost cowardly.

"You have to start somewhere," Gunnar countered.

Then, one evening, Étienne found *him*. A boy not much older than himself, slipping into the hayloft with the careless grace of someone in love. Soon, a girl followed, skirts rustling, and Étienne stayed close enough to hear the soft laughter and the muffled sounds of their pleasure. He blushed as he listened, burning with shame and hunger both.

The girl left first. The loft smelled of their lovemaking, sweet and animal, hay crushed flat beneath them. The young man lay half-undressed in the straw, one arm tucked lazily behind his head. Peaceful, radiant, so vividly alive.

He was strong, stronger than Étienne expected, and nearly wrestled him to the ground. It might have ended there, Étienne broken, his hunger unanswered, but Gunnar was watching. Coalescing from the dark, he retrieved a knife from his belt and pressed it into Étienne's hand. Étienne's fingers trembled so badly he nearly dropped it.

"Do it now."

And Étienne obeyed. His hands shook so badly that he cut himself in the frenzy. He almost brought his own bleeding wrist to taste before Gunnar stopped him.

I told Étienne how I'd reacted to consuming my own blood earlier that day.

You learned the hard way. We cannot drink from ourselves or each other. Our kind is poison to itself. Only the living will do, he said.

Our kind, I considered.

I pondered over his love story with Gunnar. I saw Gunnar in Etienne's memory, through Étienne's eyes—the way he looked at the boy, so gentle. I'd never seen Gunnar show so much affection. Not to Ophelia, anyway.

Sylvie's eyes had long since been drained of love for me, too. We put all our money into the house, only for her to realize she didn't want any of that. And she didn't want me. But I wasn't a toy to be played with and discarded when she grew bored. Nor was Whitmore!

This was supposed to have been our haven. I had wanted to keep her here with me. If we kept renovating, I thought she might eventually fall in love with me again. That had been the plan.

I'd done my research and started small. I peeled back wallpaper and tucked damp scraps and potato peels into the corners where they would spread like disease. I worked my way outside as well. I got a bag of coarse salt and spread it along the perimeter of the house, pressing it into the mortar between the stones.

I knew at least one of these things would work. I just needed a little mold, one crack, anything to keep the house from selling. Keep us renovating. Keep Sylvie with me.

I turned it over in my mind for the rest of the night while Gunnar and Ophelia held their blood feast.

The newest victim had long, heavy, curly black hair. We were not identical, but certain features echoed me. Her face had the same narrowness, the same quiet severity around the mouth, similar eyes, though I couldn't tell the color. I pretended not to notice.

Ophelia tortured her with passion. She moved slowly, prolonging each moment, drawing gasps from the woman in small, merciless thefts, savoring each tear, each scream.

My hands slid across Gunnar's and Ophelia's bodies. Our limbs tangled together, knees pressing, wrists caught, weights shifting. It felt disturbingly natural.

Étienne had told me our blood was poison. Yet when I slit Ophelia's throat, she did not die. She must have swallowed some of her own blood. Why had she not died?

"Agatha!" The mention of my new name pulled me back, and I automatically continued to move, to suck, to lick, to kiss, serving as part of this bloodied machine.

Agatha. The name pulsed in my temples like a flesh-eating worm.

I wondered whether Ophelia had once been someone else, too.

For several nights, she shifted between lunging at me and nagging Gunnar. She demanded my presence, my hands, my mouth. I stayed with her, let her caress me, listened as she complained about Gunnar, about me, about the bones.

Sitting on the floor at her feet, I watched us in the mirror— two ghostly figures suspended in the glass. Her knees pressed lightly into my back as she drew the brush through my hair. The bristles scraped my scalp in long, luxurious strokes. For a moment, I closed my eyes and drifted, but then her tone turned low and edged. Threatening.

"I feel like I am just another one of his bones." She pulled harder, and I winced. "Not a partner. Just something he keeps around until someone better comes along, and then he can add me to his collection." She let out a bitter laugh. "Maybe then he'll pay me some attention."

She gathered a section of my hair, ran her fingers through it, then set the brush aside, twisting the strands between her hands like rope. "He never stopped missing Étienne. Did you know that? I see it in the way he goes quiet. In the way he stares at the walls, like he is listening for a voice that's no longer there."

The brush dragged through another tangle, harder this time. My eyes watered.

"He loved Étienne. Sometimes I think he even prefers you. As though the two of you share a secret."

She knows, I thought. *She knows.*

She yanked so hard my head jerked back. In the mirror, her eyes caught mine.

"And when he touches you—" She leaned closer, her lips warm against my ear. "When he looks at you, Agatha, I see it. That hunger. He is not thinking of me at all. And that"—her fingers tightened in my hair, lifting my chin higher—"is the problem."

I needed to escape.

The house had grown colder as winter approached. A few windows had pulped and collapsed inward. Even in that dull gray light of day, I still could not go outside. At night, I was under constant watch.

Suspicious, Ophelia ventured out more and more seldom and almost never returned with anyone. The few prey she brought back were subtle and easy. They squirmed, and she was ravenous, her games crueler now, designed only to inflict as much pain as possible.

She fought Gunnar and me for sustenance. Me, because she could, and Gunnar, to see whether he would yield or battle. She wanted Gunnar's devotion, but it was already slipping from her grasp, and she did not see that I was the one holding it now. The acrimony between them was as loud as the bones in Whitmore.

"He's mine!" she snarled, blood flying from her mouth.

Gunnar stared at her, contemplating, and I wondered whether he wanted her around at all. Then he stepped back without a word, and I heard the floor creak above us as he retreated to his sanctuary of bones.

After that, Ophelia watched Gunnar and me like a hawk during our blood-soaked games, her eyes fixed and suspicious. Gunnar felt it too. He no longer touched me in front of her. But when we were alone, he always claimed me.

Ophelia must have sensed as much, because she stopped going out to hunt altogether. She skipped one night, then another, then a week. The hunger became overwhelming.

That night, they left together—Gunnar behind the wheel, Ophelia beside him, shining like a newly polished diamond, happy they were together. She even kissed me on the lips, promising to bring me something nice. I noticed she wasn't wearing Sylvie's clothes. She was wearing mine: jeans, a horror-movie T-shirt, right down to the heavy Dr. Martens on her feet. It made her look so young, like a teenager—her subtle frame swallowed in the oversized tee.

And then they left in the car Sylvie and I had shared since we had to sell mine.

Now was the time.

I needed to leave before Ophelia came undone. Before she and Gunnar reconciled and traced their undoing back to the venomous snake in their garden of affection—me.

I pushed the door open, and the cool night air rushed over me like a baptism. It smelled like rain and woodsmoke, dead leaves and fresh linen, so unlike the house, which withered more each day. I inhaled greedily, like an addict getting their fix. The night belonged to me now. I stepped onto the porch. Barefoot, nightgown clinging to me, I didn't care about the cold. I didn't care about anything except freedom.

One step became two. Then I sprinted. The slimy grass slapped at my ankles, the earth sucking me in, but I didn't stop. I bolted for the trees that circled the property. Beyond them lay the state park, miles and miles of forest. If I ran all night, maybe I would reach people.

All that mattered was that I was no longer inside that house.

I ran hard, lungs tearing, legs flying. The trees blurred, slick with rain, the forest opening to consume me. But then my steps faltered, each stride grew heavier than the last.

I pushed harder. The ground tilted. I stumbled, gagging, the sour heat of my stomach climbing my throat.

I tried again—another step, another gasp. I collapsed to my knees, clutching at the clammy earth, trying to force myself forward. The harder I fought, the worse it got. My vision pulsed black at the edges. I convulsed, heaving, spitting blood.

Half-faint, I crawled back toward the house.

And then—relief.

My chest loosened, and air rushed back. By the time I reached the porch again, the sickness had already ebbed.

The house took me back with open arms.

I was missing something. There had to be a way for me to leave. Gunnar and Ophelia traveled constantly. Why couldn't I?

I sobbed when I told Étienne about it. He had been unusually silent that day.

When he finally spoke, he told me how much he missed home. He painted a vivid image in my mind: the quaint cottages, flowers in bloom, the lush, rolling fields, the endless horizon, and the sun! Oh, he missed the sun most of all.

We used to take the soil from our home with us. Helvig's voice caressed me. *On our travels and conquests. To make sure we would always return home. Alive.*

It was the same thing Étienne had shared with me. It hadn't occurred to me then that he was speaking of me, too—that I wasn't just listening to stories, but to my own unmaking.

Ophelia and Gunnar had done the same, wearing the soil around their necks. I had wondered, then, if I could take some soil from Sylvie's grave, pack it into a small jar, and keep it close. If that could serve as a promise to come back. If it could allow me to leave.

I wondered what eternity would be like, when the world had already rejected you long before you became the thing that plagued the night. Would one get a job? Steal? Wander the streets, feeding on people who were already forgotten? What would one do with the opportunity to live forever—or at least as long as Gunnar?

He was ancient. He had seen the world gather itself from nothing, crumble in wars, and rebuild again. He had seen continents discovered, empires rise and crumble. He had watched fire become industry, and industry become light. He had lived through Copernicus mapping the heavens, through the first plague that swept Europe, through the Reformation tearing faith apart, through the French Revolution drowning the streets in red. He watched the trenches of the Great War fill with boys who still smelled of milk. He saw men walk on the moon. And still, he remained there, hiding from daylight in a crumbling house, surrounded by the bones of his dead lovers.

XIV

In their lair, lay the earth from their motherlands. They couldn't go without it. It fed them, restored them, soothed them. Just as the ground kept fossils intact for centuries, the earth kept them preserved. *Immortal.*

The bones never told me whether it had to be soil from where I lived or where I was born.

I was born elsewhere, yet this house had become my home. Perhaps that was why I couldn't leave. I had to carry the soil, like emotional baggage, wherever I went.

Étienne, Helvig, Isolde, Francesco, and the others watched me, their smiles fixed in sadness and silent anticipation. I didn't tell them what I was about to do, but I felt they knew. And they judged me for betraying someone who had allowed me to live, who cared for me, though in such a perverse way.

I was a traitor, about to bite the hand that fed me.

Sylvie.

So much had changed since we last spoke, and I needed her now more than ever. I needed to tell her that I no longer knew who I was, that I didn't know who I wanted or needed to become. I needed to tell her how desperately I wanted her back.

If only she had still been alive.

But it didn't matter. Two days before her death, she told me she wanted to separate. To live apart for a while. She said she'd found a studio to rent. She no longer cared about the house or the money; she just wanted to get away from me.

When people said they wanted to separate, it meant they wanted to leave. It was only a softer word, an illusion that things might still mend themselves. But what it actually meant was that they were done with you. Even if they would not admit it, even to themselves.

And when Gunnar and Ophelia appeared, I believed the universe had answered my prayers, because I didn't know what else to do. I summoned them, my demons of resolution, to pull me out of the ruins of self-destruction. And they did.

They killed Sylvie, yes.

But Sylvie, you were done with me before you were done with life. And somehow, losing you to death felt easier than losing you to someone else.

Rochelle's body was, quite literally, a dead weight over my shoulders.

Ophelia and Gunnar's relationship felt like walking through a minefield. Yes, they both were prone to pulling me to their sides, but when it came down to it, they would choose each other, and I would be cast aside.

I needed to seek help outside of our ménage à trois.

And when I ran, I would need protection. I had to pin Rochelle's death on Ophelia. She could have done it. She was violent, merciless, always ravenous. Gunnar knew this.

Ergo, I had needed to dispose of Rochelle's body the same way they had made me bury everyone else.

I had so little time. Hours had passed; Gunnar and Ophelia would be back soon.

I ran downstairs, a flickering candle in hand. A wave of carrion crashed into me as I yanked open the closet door. The air reeked of burst intestines and liquefying organs. Gases from Rochelle's decomposing physique bulged against the DIY body bag. Worst of all, her face, distorted now, was pressed against the plastic, still staring at me with a suppurating, judgmental glare.

I looked away, unable to withstand the sight. Overcoming a surge of vile revulsion, I wrapped her in my arms and dragged the crinkling, squishing form out. Faster and faster I went across the hall, while the slick rustle made my skin crawl.

An erratic, high-speed thrumming took over my chest. My mouth was so dry that when I tried to swallow, my throat seized, refusing to acknowledge the command.

I reached the door, my hand trembling as I pushed it open. And . . .

There, at the threshold, stood Ophelia.

Her face was pale in the lamplight. Beside her stood a middle-aged man dressed in a coat too thin for the rain. I knew the type. They worked dead-end retail jobs and swooned over models, male and female, online—begging to be humiliated while their lonely lives passed them by and their hairlines made a slow retreat. He was both pathetic and sad. His dull eyes widened when he saw me, sweaty and disheveled.

"What the hell is this?" Ophelia asked.

I gasped, my chest rising and falling in desperate bursts. No reasonable answer, no clever lie would come. The man behind Ophelia instinctively moved back, but he was not fast enough to escape the visceral anger Ophelia had intended for me. Her hand shot out. It looked as if she had pulled the knife from thin air, and before he could blink, she drove the blade through his throat.

His panic became a frantic struggle as his fingers clawed, and he collapsed forward with a sodden crump.

Her attention was back on me. It was my turn now.

"What are you doing, Agatha?"

I let go of the edges of the makeshift bag. The body pooled around me.

Behind Ophelia, another shadow approached. Gunnar did not even glance at the corpses. With his heavy gaze, he assessed the situation and turned to Ophelia.

She didn't say anything, just lifted an eyebrow gently in an expression that said, *I have no idea.* I thought she would tell him that she had found me like that, with a cadaver, but she just stood there in silence. Only her eyes were glinting, as if she had hoped to catch me in a precarious position—and finally, I offered her that grace.

Gunnar had the same influence on her as she had on me. Love and fear. The beginning and the end.

"I told you: not like the last time," he said, punctuating every word.

It looked like he was going to hit her, but his hand shot toward me instead. The slap came so fast I didn't see it, I only felt the sting bloom across my cheek, white-hot and deep. I fell, knocked down over two dead bodies.

Gunnar passed me without a backward glance, disappearing into the house. Ophelia slowly shook her head. Her arms were crossed over her chest, the knife still primed in her right hand.

"Now you've done it, Agatha."

Ophelia gestured for me to follow, and I obeyed, leaving the dead in their different stages of decay. She waved me toward the open door that led to the basement. From the heaviness in the air, I knew Gunnar was waiting for me there.

"I'm going to take a bath," she announced, and she started upstairs, shedding my clothes from her back with lazy contempt.

I moved beyond the basement where Gunnar waited beside

the soil-filled coffins. I stopped in front of them, and he stood right behind me.

"Touch the soil," he growled.

I did. It was ice-cold beneath my fingers. So cold that I nearly felt the sting of frostbite, and I instinctively pulled away.

"It is cold, isn't it?"

He approached and put his hand into the box on the left. He let the dirt sift through his fingers as if it were silk.

"It feels warm to me because it is my place of rest."

He turned back to me, grazing my hand as he pointed to the second box.

"This is Ophelia's." He opened it to reveal fecund earth that looked welcoming and rich.

Gunnar traced the edge of the wood, though he did not touch the dirt inside.

"Feel it."

I swallowed, caught between fear and a crepuscular urge. Ophelia's bed of soil was even colder than Gunnar's.

"Your own bed will feel good. It will feel like home wherever you go."

My own bed. The cellar held these two boxes, and there was no space for a third. He didn't say it aloud, but I understood the implication.

There was no room for anyone else here. For me to have a place, someone had to go.

He caught my chin, and only then did I see the blade in his hand. He pressed it lightly against my cheek.

"Blood is shared, and dead bodies belong in the ground. Understand?"

I shivered at the closeness of him. The blade moved, slow enough that I could feel the exact moment the skin parted. Blood welled at once, warm, almost ticklish as it traced the curve of my cheek. I held still, offering the small obedience he required.

I knew what this was. Punishment, yes, but it felt almost ceremonial. Consensual.

And in his eyes, trepidation. Admiration. *Love?*

This was how he had looked at Étienne, too.

The blood, the pain, it was not for him. It was not for me.

It was for Ophelia.

Once he was done, he shut Ophelia's box with a gentle finality and pushed me to sit on top of it. The cold edge pressed through the fabric of my nightgown. The candelabra fell, the flames vanished, enveloping us in an artificial night.

He lowered himself between my legs. The scent of him, earthy and metallic, filled my senses. I gasped, and he took the sound in, letting it guide him. His mouth found me.

It was almost too much—his closeness and his greed. He went deeper, harder, moving with a knowledge of my body that made me tremble. My hands clawed at the edge of Ophelia's box, my nails digging into the case to the soft, squelching sounds of him devouring me.

I gave in.

XV

When Ophelia saw the cut, she didn't smirk or speak. A strange flicker in her eyes hinted at something other than celebration, though I struggled to pinpoint the emotion. She dampened a towel and wiped the blood from my cheek. Unlike our usual encounters, the gesture held no sexual connotation. She looked at me with something closer to pity. The cut looked worse than it felt.

Had Gunnar punished her as well? He must have. I wondered in what ways. The only time I'd seen her broken was when I slit her throat, yet that wound had long since vanished.

She cast one last look at me and drifted downstairs, retreating into her box without a word. Left in this invidious silence, I struggled against a sudden, unwanted ache of sympathy for her. She had been only a child when she was married off, and then broken. Then she was taken—*saved?*—by Gunnar, and forged into something new.

I languished in bed and pondered the possibility that I needed to be placed in the soil, too. What did that mean for me? What had I become?

The following evening, Ophelia slipped out to hunt. Gunnar occupied the time in his room with his collection of bones, leaving me without a chance to speak to either of them or ask what I should do.

But with Gunnar, we shared a reticent agreement, and tonight was the night.

I had hoped for more time. Perhaps Ophelia would stay out until there was no time left at all, just enough to satiate herself and play a little before dawn forced an end to it.

Don't come home, don't come home.

But she was efficient this time. She returned before the hour had even turned, bringing with her a man who looked in his early twenties.

She'd brought women only a few times. It had nothing to do with the way they tasted. I assumed men were easier, more eager to follow a stranger into the night, chasing the promise of pleasure in the sleepless hours. Usually, she chose older prey—in their fifties or sixties who were easily drawn to her beauty and her eternal youth that hovered right on the edge of the age of consent. They were so drunk on it they grew careless. They also tended to carry more cash; the older the man, the thicker the wad of paper bills in his wallet.

She once told me, laughing, that she didn't even lie to them. She told them, "I will eat you alive," and they followed, led by their eager manhood. And then she did—just not in the way they imagined.

This one was blond and tall, almost handsome, though his face was equine in a way that made him look perpetually uncertain.

Ophelia led him into the room, kissing him as she removed his jacket, then his shirt. He was so entranced by her that he noticed nothing. Not the stains in the carpet. Not the damp metallic air. Perhaps he was drunk. Perhaps she had already begun working her quiet influence on him.

She pushed him onto the bed, and I watched from the corner, hidden in shadow. I could see them clearly. He exhaled sharply as he fell back, his eyes caught in the gravity of her presence. The silk dress slipped from her shoulders, sliding down her body in one slow motion. She nudged it aside with the tip of her toe.

The boy fumbled with his clothes, urgency clinging to every movement. She watched him with mild-interest, her attention already elsewhere, already anticipating the next phase of her design.

When his clothes joined hers, she moved over him with a strange tenderness, each gesture deliberate, almost reverent, as though enacting a ritual older than either of them.

Hovering above him, she paused for a long moment. Then she lifted her eyes to me. The look was brief, but unmistakable. I nodded to her. Only then did she lower herself onto him. Her lashes quivered as she steadied herself.

Their movements quickly grew erratic. She gripped the bedpost with one hand, red hair spilling over her shoulders and down her back. In the wavering candlelight, she seemed almost unreal, a figure carved from sex and sin.

He held her hips, guiding her, unable to look anywhere but at her. I knew the hypnosis of her beauty—the way she made you feel like there was no one else in the world. But some beautiful things existed only to be destroyed, and perhaps their beauty lay precisely in their fleetingness.

Her gaze flickered toward me once more. I understood. I had learned to read her silences. I knew her well.

I took a step forward from the corner where I had stood the entire time. I circled them, and Ophelia closed her eyes, trusting me. I approached, shedding my nightgown. I placed the knife beside their bodies, sliding it into the bloodied sheets, and then climbed onto the bed and held Ophelia from behind.

"What the fuck?" the man mumbled, growing aware of my presence. "Who is she?"

But he was already too far gone. Ophelia did not stop moving, and soon he didn't seem to mind the presence of two of us.

A cold current. That was how I knew Gunnar was there, too. That was how I knew it was time.

I slid my hand into the sheets, retrieved the knife, and pressed it lightly against Ophelia's chest. I let the blade trace down her skin, slow enough to raise a shiver in its wake.

At the same moment, the man reached his end. His face tightened as release overtook him. He groaned and came inside her, one hand gripping her hip while the other squeezed her right breast.

That was when I slashed his throat.

He gurgled, hands flying upward, but I withdrew the knife almost immediately.

Ophelia bent over and latched onto his neck, working as the man convulsed beneath her.

Gunnar came closer and lowered himself onto the bed, preparing to drink.

Fresh blood stirred my hunger, and I swallowed hard to resist.

Now.

I had to do it now.

The man between Ophelia's thighs was alive but weakening.

"Gunnar?"

He raised his face to look at me, hearing me speak for what seemed like the first time ever. And I lowered the knife once more.

Unlike our guest, Gunnar did not yelp.

When the knife went into his left eye, he growled like an injured animal, dragging us both from the bed as he slammed me into the floor. The air fled me in a broken rasp. Pinning me by the throat with one hand, he gripped the handle of the weapon, wrenching the blade out of his eye before flinging it somewhere behind him. His spit struck my cheek. Blood was pouring out of him, and I squeezed my mouth shut to avoid catching a drop.

Ophelia was easy to understand. She took because someone had taken from her. It was all she had ever known. But Gunnar was a different kind of beast. He enjoyed it: the blood, the suffering, the death. The owning. He thought he owned everything and everyone—and he did. Just like I had looked at Sylvie and thought I owned her. We were so much alike, he and I.

Perhaps this is why his gift of talking to the dead was passed to me.

But two of the same kind can never coexist.

And in Gunnar's eyes, I read everything. Regret. Fury.

I didn't deserve to live.

Despite his wound, he pinned me to the floor, his weight crashing down on me. He would take my body apart, and I wouldn't resist.

I closed my eyes and stilled myself.

A hiss of silk tickled my face as a fresh weight fell over me.

Ophelia. Fighting for me!

She grabbed her silk dress and used it like a rope, strangling Gunnar to try and pull him off me.

I thought she kept me to punish me for almost killing her, but it was the opposite. She clung to me because I took from her.

In a world where men had always carved pieces from her, she didn't know how to recognize a hand that wasn't a fist. When she saw me do the same, she naturally latched on. I was simply the next strong thing to claim her.

She was mine.

Ophelia straddled Gunnar's back, her face tense, teeth bared. And then she drove the blade into his heart from behind.

She forced the knife deeper. Gunnar roared, tangled in pain and disbelief.

Our meal dragged himself from the bed. He crawled toward the door, one hand clamped to his neck, trying to hold himself together. Lost to the noise and motion, I only turned back when it was already too late. Gunnar had torn free from Ophelia's grip. Somehow, he had wrenched the knife from his back and driven it into my thigh.

I roared. He tore the blade free, ready to end it, but I twisted away with what strength remained. I crashed into the man's body. He lay limp beneath me, unresponsive, already emptied. Life had abandoned him before he could escape the chaos.

His penis brushed my leg, soft and inert.

Gunnar lunged, and I dragged myself backward. He stumbled over the corpse I had just fallen across.

"No!"

With that cry, Ophelia leapt on him once more. Without hesitation, he caught her by the hair and slit her throat. Not the clumsy tearing I had done that first night, but a clean slice from side to side. Blood filled her mouth, her body turned against itself as her own vitality entered her system.

"Oh . . ." she croaked, trying to stifle the flow.

I searched the floor blindly, fingers striking fabric, buttons, damp folds of clothing. Nothing. Nothing that could be used.

Then I found it.

The Stanley knife. The same one Ophelia had used on Sylvie, on me, on so many others.

In one motion, I drove it upward—no aiming, no overthinking, guided only by speed and panic—straight into Gunnar's second eye. He howled, clutching at the ruins of his face as he tried to reach me.

That was when Ophelia, one hand still at her throat, forced the second knife into his chest.

Blinded, Gunnar dropped to his knees.

She did not stop.

Minutes passed. Ophelia struck again and again, keening in grief.

I was screaming too. The sound swallowed everything, a miasma of noise, alive inside the room. And then I joined her in the frantic unmaking of the man who'd made us.

We cut and stabbed, cut and stabbed, cut and stabbed. Flesh tore. Skin split. Fragments of him fell to the floor.

The world around us drowned in red, and the bones upstairs wept.

We didn't stop until Gunnar's body convulsed once, twice, and then collapsed inward, emptied of structure. Ophelia stepped back, as if waking from a trance, awareness returning all at once. The knife slipped from her hold.

I paused, numb, not because I didn't understand what we had done, but because I didn't know what she would do next.

They had been together for nearly a hundred years. Was that enough time for love to fester into contempt, or did something remain, buried under habit and shared survival? Was she mourning him, regretting the moment she chose to take me in? Or perhaps killing him was like cutting out a malignancy only to discover it had spread everywhere; to get rid of him fully, she would have to cut out every part of herself.

I moved toward her, intending to guide her back to her lair, to let her recover in the soil of her homeland. But she shook her head in a pained "no."

Through clenched teeth, she said, "We need to bury him."

She had taken his dirt-filled medallion. Nothing left for him to anchor himself to, nothing that could sustain him. I looked at the hemorrhage she had become. If she didn't get into her soil soon, she'd be beyond saving.

Ophelia noticed my hesitation. "We need to make sure, Agatha."

The pendant at her throat held only a fragment of soil. It wouldn't sustain her for long. And yet, she refused to leave me.

Burying him was not enough for her. She made me fetch the hatchet Sylvie and I had used to split wood from the living room.

I placed the blade at Gunnar's shoulder and swung.

The steel bit, skin splitting, the muscle resisting with a strange elasticity. He emitted a congested, gurgling sound, more a vibration than a voice, like a corpse stirring in its own skin. I stumbled back, sweat slick on my forehead.

I hacked at the legs. Bone grated, metal bit. I slid the hatchet along his femur, following the curve, the blade meeting resistance before snapping through.

The entire time, Ophelia sat in the corner. She was still naked, still covered in blood, still gripping the knife, staring into space, probably trying to visualize what her life would be now, without him. Remembering who she was before.

I had only been with them for a few months, but I couldn't remember myself either. My life before them felt like a series of pictures in someone else's album, all out of order. Thinking beyond this moment, beyond the blade splintering the bone, was more effort than I was willing to give.

I took his head last. His remaining eye still watched me. It only took a few chops to decapitate him fully. I heaved, then dragged the sheet from the bed and started placing the body parts on top.

I would have to make two or three trips. Gunnar, now just a heap of pieces and gore stacked upon a sheet, was bigger than anyone I'd ever seen. It was hard to believe he was truly gone.

His presence, once so enormous, was seeping out of the house like an exorcism.

The grave I dug was wide and shallow, but it took most of the night to finish. Like I had felt trying to enter the forest, the garden seemed to refuse Gunnar, rejecting him as a creature of another time and place.

I dug. I dug. I dug. Just as I had that first night. Just as I had when I buried Sylvie.

In the hour before sunrise, Ophelia's figure emerged from the house, wavering like smoke. She'd wrapped herself in one of Sylvie's old trench coats.

"Wait," she said, pulling a salt shaker from one of the pockets. "He did it once. To the one before me."

Even though the soil was no longer his and couldn't sustain him, Ophelia did not take the chance.

When I was a child, it was a local legend: an envious neighbor contaminating a more successful farmer's field with salt to make the soil infertile.

There was so little left in the shaker that I could hear the granules rattling from where I stood. She knelt at the edge of the grave and scattered the grains. They winked like tiny diamonds.

A pale strand of light spread across the horizon, sharpening the mist and turning the air brittle. I wondered if Ophelia had always hated him but never allowed herself to admit it. And what did that make of me? Was I only a vessel, something to steady herself against? Perhaps she, like him, had feared the length of eternity, and together they had wound around each other like toxic vines—beautiful and suffocating, draining whatever they touched.

Sylvie had been scared to leave me, too, and chose to find a replacement, someone to distract her so there was no void when she finally departed. She had been waiting for Rochelle to return so she could take the final step and sever the dead limb —me.

Or was it a much simpler equation? Ophelia feared Gunnar would replace her with me, so she struck before she could become another quiet relic in his keeping.

I lowered Gunnar's pieces into the grave, and Ophelia poured soil over them. Then I dragged the young man forward and placed him beside Gunnar.

Something about it felt wrong. Gunnar had lived too long, had gathered too much knowledge from the world to be reduced to this. Yet he had never existed alone, moving from one companion to another, binding them to him. Now he would remain beside a man whose name we never learned.

The first faint blush of morning spread across the sky as I pressed the earth flat. My heart beat too fast. My teeth would not stop chattering.

"We did it, Agatha. It's done."

Agatha.

In some deep, innocent ignorance, like Ophelia, I had hoped to reclaim the lost part of myself.

Yet, there I was, still the same, with no past and no present.

Ophelia and I stumbled back toward the house.

I supported her as best I could, her strength fading, yet she refused the respite that would have healed her. She stayed beside me. Loyal, as she once was to Gunnar.

I guided her to the basement and helped her into her box. Before I could put the lid on, she looked at me. For a moment, I thought she understood everything. Then she gave a faint smile and closed her eyes. I looked at her ethereal face, marked with drying blood, and lowered the lid.

The next night, when I return to Ophelia, only a skeleton wearing a bloodied gown remains. Fragments of decay cling to old bones, and pale threads of softened tissue slide between them.

The reason Ophelia never found more salt was simple: I had used it all. Before she came home, I mixed a whole box of salt into her soil and made sure it wasn't viable.

Now, the earth that once restored her was a corrosive nest of her own demise.

I gather her bones carefully into an empty box. They seem to reach toward me, calling silently.

Agatha. Agatha.

Ashamed, I don't answer. Ophelia saved me. She welded me into who I was now. Though what she possessed wasn't love. It was a hungry, biting limerence. A fever, rather than a feeling.

But I couldn't bear leaving her there, in the cold cellar of the house. She deserved rest.

After burying her beneath the skeletal husks of the hydrangea, the same ones she had admired that first night, I return to the room of bones. They regard me in silence. No last words wait there, no confessions, no pleas. I carry each bone outside as gently as I can and bury them one by one. I plant them like seeds.

Each placement takes time. Hours pass, but I don't hurry. The labor steadies me even as it hurts. It feels like parting from companions who have been there for me in the worst of times.

When I finish, the house of bones stands empty. It watches in silence, stripped of its burden. And after so long, it's quiet. No voices, no whispers.

That night, I bring some soil inside with me. I scatter it across my bed and lie down in it. I expect revulsion, but a deep sleep takes me immediately. When I wake, I feel restored. Resurrected. The wounds on my thighs have begun to close, and flecks of soil cling to the healing skin like ointment.

There is still more to do. I take the shovel and go out again.

I cross the grounds, find the unmarked plot, and kneel by it.

Sylvie's grave with the old gazebo leaning precariously over it.

Starvation twists through me as I dig. I plan to venture into town soon, find someone, and bring them back before setting off for good. One last death to gift Whitmore.

At last, the smell of decay reaches me, sweet and foul enough to make me retch. I cover my mouth. Her hair appears first. It chokes my fingers. Patches of waxen tissue still bind it to her skull. I thought I might need to break it free, but it has already separated. Relief washes over me, knowing I don't have to cause any further harm to what remains of her.

My love.

And after all these months, she is with me again.

I carry her skull back into the house and give it a thorough wash. When it's clean, I dry it and take it upstairs.

I place her on the shelf and sit beside it, watching, waiting for her to respond.

And eventually, she does.

THE END

ACKNOWLEDGMENTS

Victoria Iva for the beautiful artwork that became this book's cover

Lyuba Rybakova for the cover layout, design, and her unwavering faith in this project

Kara Jordan for her meticulous editing and for pouring her heart and soul into this text

My family for being so supportive, even though I asked them not to read this particular book

My husband for supporting me in every way possible

ABOUT THE AUTHOR

DG Woods has been haunted by nightmares and sleep paralysis since childhood. But instead of letting her demons take dominion, she's turned the tables, bared her fangs and reshaped them into stories that she calls "dark and just real enough to make you question reality".

When she's not hounding her monsters or turning their antics into stories, she can be found hiding in the woods somewhere on the East Coast with her family, making spooky photos and videos.

BOOKS BY DG WOODS

Explore other works of D.G. Woods:

Into the Dark, We Go

A witchy Appalachian mystery.

Fairbanks

A dystopian novella about a family at the end of the world.